AND DEATH SHALL HAVE NO DOMINION: TALES OF THE TITANIC

AND DEATH SHALL HAVE NO DOMINION: TALES OF THE TITANIC

Edited by Dean M. Drinkel

Dean M. Drinkel/ Lycopolis Press

AND DEATH SHALL HAVE NO DOMINION: TALES OF THE TITANIC

ISBN-13: 978-1512072945
ISBN-10: 51207294X

Lycopolis Press
www.lycopolispress.co.uk

"The storm made bliss of my sea-borne awakenings. Lighter than a cork, I danced on the waves which men call eternal rollers of victims..."
Arthur Rimbaud, The Drunken Boat

"There is no danger that Titanic will sink. The boat is unsinkable and nothing but inconvenience will be suffered by the passengers."
Philip Franklin, White Star Line Vice President

"Let them curse it that curse the day, who are ready to raise up their mourning."
Job 3:8

For
Chris Hardman
George Henry White

CONTENTS

EDITOR'S NOTE

Please note, in the stories that follow, the Author's original spelling and intention has been retained depending upon their nationality (i.e. through / thru etc).

FOREWORD

I'll keep this simple as I'd really like the stories that follow to speak for themselves and you don't want me droning on about this or that, but I will say this: compiling and editing this anthology has been both a pleasure and an honour.

The original concept came about initially because I'd always wanted to mark the anniversary of the Titanic's sinking in one or another and after discussing it with some fellow writers I decided that "And Death Shall Have No Dominion" could be such a fitting tribute.

I wanted also to keep the anthology as tight, manageable and personable as possible and literally only asked the writers who I had had those original discussions with – luckily for me they all said yes (and very quickly too). There wasn't a word count as such, no hard and fast rules about what the stories could / could not contain as long as the Titanic was involved somewhere along the line.

I believe I chose wisely and was not left wanting, which I hope goes for you too Gentle Reader as you turn the pages and see what this talented bunch have dreamt up for you.

So with that in mind, I'll stop now because as I say, I want you to dive inside as soon as you can – after all you've spent your hard earned cash to purchase it, so who am I to stop you?

Finally then, whilst I obviously thank them for their contributions, Lycopolis Press for publishing the anthology, James Powell for a wonderful (as always!) cover art and you Gentle Reader for buying this book, I would like to take a couple of moments of your time for personally thanking the following:

Kristin; Dave N; Bernard G; Scott N; Kim T; Nicola M; Martin D; Ricky W; Vincent; Christophe; Stephan; Thomas; Emile; Gary; Tom & Dustin; Sia; Abi Titmuss; Tom; Don; Bradley, James, Tris and Con; Justin B; Martin B; Sam; Nile; Danny; Dan; Karis, Joe, Sheena; Elizabeth Fraser; Devon Sawa; Ronan Farrow; Cole & Dylan; Mark West; Paul Woodward; Paul Kane; Jim McLeod; Peter Mark May; Suzanne Kendall; Ed Ward; Graham Townsend; Marilyn Manson; Madonna; Tom Carroll; Harry Winks; Lewis Holtby; Mario Götze; Jack Grealish; Rob & Sheri; Barbie Wilde; Dean & Rosanna; Dianna Ippolito; Niven, Janine, Emily & Sarah; Nigel, Sinead, Zac & Alex; Simon, Harri & Charley; Mater; SJR.

Love to you all
Dean M. Drinkel
London May 2015

AND THE BAND PLAYED ON

by Nerine Dorman

The mellow tones of The Doors' *Riders on the Storm* seeped through my awareness of only the pixels on the screen that I rearranged then modified again.

Only then did I figure out what was wrong - the music competed with what already offered me sonic thrills.

Not a great track for a ring tone but I couldn't help myself.

"Fuck."

It was twenty past two in the fucking morning.

Saturday morning to be precise. Who the fuck phoned someone at this time? With dread visions of death, accident or drama, I hit save, minimized the screen and put iTunes on mute.

Neill.

What the fuck?

I hadn't heard from him for months, not since the breakup. I hesitated before I pressed answer. It wasn't like him to drunk-dial ex-girlfriends.

"Hello?"

"You have to help me!" It was a woman.

"What? Who's this?" What the hell was Neill up to?

"Please!" she sobbed.

"Are you crazy, lady?" It then struck me that this could possibly be a genuine emergency. Maybe something had happened to Neill beyond getting his cellphone stolen.

She sucked in a gulp of breath and didn't speak for a good five seconds. "You're Anja, right?" Her tone was shaky.

"Ja, what of it? Why don't you tell me what's happening?"

"I..." She exhaled and another long silence stretched out. "I'm a friend. Of Neill's. I'm looking after his house for him. He's...gone away on a trip but there's been an emergency and I've got to leave. He said if there were any problems that I should call you."

Now that was weird. She sounded like she was reading off a script, and her accent was funny. Irish. "He did?"

"He said you'd understand."

That was so typical of Neill. When we'd been seeing each other, he'd had a bad habit of making his problems my problems - part of the reason why we'd split - but to lump me with his issues after the breakup...

Now that was just plain weird.

Especially after all this time with no contact.

I rubbed my face and blew out. "When will he be back?"

"Um, in...a week?"

"Right." For the first time exhaustion sank its claws into my body. Sixteen straight hours at my desk. I needed to get some rest. "What time can I come by tomorrow...sorry, later today?"

"Please can you come now?" Little girl lost.

"It's like almost half-past two in the morning. Can't it wait?"

"It can't wait. I must go as soon as possible."

A yawn all but split my face and I shook my head. I contemplated the wind sluicing rain against my windows. I'd have to go out in that. "Don't you have friends?" I knew I sounded heartless but at this point I couldn't be arsed.

"I'm new in town. Please, Anja. You're the only one Neill said I could trust with his place."

As if.

I snorted though I'd rather punch at the wall, at the table - break something. Knowing Neill, he was such a misfit I had been the only woman stupid enough to put up with his shit to make it as far as crossing over the threshold of his lair.

Mausoleum, rather.

The guy had some sick fascination with the Titanic, and frankly, the place gave me the heebie-jeebies. Most likely his reluctant house-sitter was chickening out due to the creepiness factor. God knows I'd struggled to go to the loo unless the lights were all on.

Most of all, I hated the prints of all those staring faces which lined the passage leading between the lounge and bedroom - photos of folks who'd survived the disaster. It was just downright freaky. They'd headed off, so many hundreds of them. And only a handful had survived.

So full of dreams, hopes for a better future.

So many dead, families and friends lost. Neill loved those pictures. I shuddered.

And the life-sized posters of Kate Winslet in period dress? Ugh.

"Anja?" The woman's piteous voice drew me back to the present. She really did sound as though she needed help.

I sighed. "Give me an hour to get my things together and I'll be there."

Neill didn't live far from me. I had my nifty little bachelor apartment in the uber-trendy Old Mutual building, in the heart of town. He had his chic art deco apartment up in Vredehoek, complete with genuine Bauhaus-era décor that probably cost more than my car.

We had that much in common - a love of retro. That hadn't been enough to keep our relationship afloat.

I copied the files I'd been working on onto my laptop, packed a few things then headed out into the stormy night. I tried to be philosophical about this small drama - in all likelihood I probably could do with a change in scenery for a few days once I'd established that Neill's damsel in distress wasn't in mortal danger.

"You're twenty-six, Anja," I muttered to myself as I strapped on the safety belt of my battered VW Golf. "You should be out partying it with your girlfriends, yet you're making pretty pictures for a steak ranch's fucking menu."

Most of my girlfriends had men, and were most likely snuggled safe in bed at this ungodly hour of the morning. I might as well have Loser tattooed across my forehead, with Geek Girl underneath for good measure.

Neill's mystery woman was waiting for me in the street when I pulled up. She huddled in an oversized trench coat that looked like it belonged to a man. Her dark curls were plastered against pale skin and her eyes were huge, luminous pools of fright. What possessed her to stand out here in the pissing rain?

She zoned in on me even before I could get out of the car, and pressed the keys into my hand. "Thank you!" Her teeth chattered and it was clear she was hyperventilating.

"Sure," I said, uncertain. "Look, have you got a ride or something?"

"I've got to go." She spun away, already across the street and out of reach.

"Hey..." I stood like an idiot, rapidly getting soaked as she ran down Buitenkant Street.

Where had I seen her before? Neill didn't have many friends but I'd met a few at his occasional dinner parties. I fumbled for a name that remained stubbornly elusive.

The sooner I got inside, the better, and I shouldered my backpack, locked the car and swore my way into Neill's apartment, which to add to my annoyance, was on the third floor of a building that didn't have an elevator.

The place was silent - and cold - and the first thing I did was turn on the gas fire while trying to avoid looking at the enormous poster featuring Leonardo DiCaprio giving cuddles to Kate.

Damn, I hated that movie.

I'd inadvertently watched it almost a dozen times by proxy, and every time I happened to see the end - I'd always tried to keep busy on my computer - I'd bawl my eyes out.

Neill would just sit there wrapped in his favorite blanket, the tears flowing freely and a stupid shit-eating grin plastered on his face.

Fucking sicko.

He repeated this routine every other weekend. We could have gone out and had social lives like normal people, but oh no, he'd rather relive the end of a doomed ship.

To give him some credit, Neill hadn't been a terminal dopehead, or languished at the local watering hole every other night with boozed-up friends and a rotten excuse for pub night quizzes, but it still didn't make up for his Titanic affliction.

His collection was impressive. He'd spent the kind of money most people would invest in a small business on acquiring genuine memorabilia related to the ill-starred liner.

Framed posters advertising the maiden voyage were preserved behind glass. He even had a display cabinet filled with surplus crockery all bearing the White Star Line's branding.

Captain Smith, dressed in his regalia, was reproduced Andy Warhol style on a giant canvas.

Neill had commissioned that one himself and I shuddered every time when I recalled how much he'd paid a local artist for the honor of screen-printing the damned thing.

Exhausted beyond all measure, I managed to drag my weary bones on a tour of the apartment. Nothing appeared to be out of place. What in the hell had that woman gotten me out for that couldn't have waited until a reasonable hour?

* * *

Rain still bucketed down later that morning when I cracked open my lids. My cellphone told me it was almost eleven yet the apartment was shrouded in gloom thanks to the thick drapes.

Blackout curtains - another of Neill's foibles.

He had a thing for fancy lighting since he didn't want to risk his collection getting damaged by UV radiation.

Well, he wasn't here now to bitch at me for pulling back the curtains. I stared morosely at the grayness outside and at the runnels of precipitation crawling down the glass before I turned around.

Footprints had been tracked on the parquet flooring. Wet footprints, as though someone had gone swimming and had stood dripping at the foot of the bed...watching me sleep.

"What the...," I stared. My skin went cold and my chest closed, and it was with great difficulty that I dragged air into my lungs. "Fuck me."

Had I locked the front door last night? I pelted down the passage to the lounge. The key was on the inside of the door, which was locked. The security chain was engaged. The footprints led from the flat screen TV that dominated the lounge.

My breath wheezed and I rubbed at my eyes. Those wet footprints didn't go away.

"Is this some sort of elaborate hoax, Neill?" I called out loudly. "It's not funny. You can come out now."

Only silence greeted me, accompanied by the rain. Hollow silence.

I wasn't given to believing in supernatural explanations but this was just fucked up. Then again, I had been tired last night. Maybe I'd been sleepwalking or something. There was that. Or maybe not. I had been absolutely soaked when I came in but I'd still been wearing shoes. These were footprints - bare feet.

I fetched the mop from the scullery and cleaned up the water. I didn't want Neill's precious parquet floor ruined. There had to be some sort of rational explanation for this bullshit.

In the meanwhile, I'd abuse his wireless internet and continue with my work. I had a deadline on Monday at eight. I simply didn't have the time to worry about stupid shit.

I set up my computer in his dining room, grabbed coffee - he always had good coffee - and started working on those illustrations.

I did at least remember to feed his bloody fish before I eventually crashed at one on Sunday morning.

The tank was there in the dining room, complete with a reproduction of the Titanic wreck at the bottom blowing bubbles out of its funnels.

I had to admit it was kind of soothing to look up once in a while to see the sharks, silver dollars and angel fish dart about. I wasn't completely alone. The added benefit was the surround sound system with its iPod dock, which did The Cure a whole lot more justice than my tinny speakers at home.

That night I dreamed I was drowning. The water was so cold it pressed all the air out of my lungs and when I screamed, it gushed down my throat. I thrashed but I could feel myself sink, my body growing leaden as I struggled for a smudge of light suspended above me in the inky water.

Down...down...down...

I sat up with a gasp then realized where I was.

Neill's bed.

And I was wet, soaked through and freezing, as though some sick fuck had just dowsed me in a bucket of frigid water.

When I licked my lips I tasted salt. Sea water.

What the fuck?

Shivers wracked my body and I peeled out of the bed and staggered to the light switch. The room exploded into brightness and I had to blink a good few seconds before I could focus.

I'd expected so see a damp patch on the bed where I'd lain only moments ago, but the bedding, although contorted, was dry.

As was I.

I licked my lips again and still tasted salt. What the fuck? Since when did I have such vivid nightmares? Cautiously I approached the bed. Nope. Not a drop of water, though my skin felt stiff with salt, as though I'd spent the day swimming in the sea.

"Bloody hell." My hands shook when I tried to call up Neill's number but his phone just rang and rang before going through to voicemail. What did I expect? It was twenty past fucking two in the morning.

Of course I couldn't go back to sleep, not after that, so I went and made myself coffee and sat blearily in the lounge, mug in hand. Rain still pissed outside, and a faint orange gleam from the streetlights oozed through a gap in the drapes. I found some vintage David Bowie on my iPod, and hoped Ziggy Stardust could pull me out of my funk.

"It's this damned place," I muttered, over and over again, mainly to convince myself. It was serious bad mojo to wallow in sick shit like the greatest maritime disaster known to man. "Neill, you're a fucking ghoul."

I could only ascribe my current bad vibes to general lack of sleep and too much stress. Neill owed me bigtime for this when he came back.

Right now I needed to focus on those damn illustrations of steaks, burgers and quesadillas then on Monday I'd call his office and see whether his boss or one of his colleagues could help me track him down so I could keel-haul his ass.

Despite the coffee, I must have dozed off because the next I knew, the strains of an all too familiar film soundtrack stirred me from my sleep.

The TV was on, and the opening scenes from *Titanic* blazed across the screen. What the hell? I must have sat on the remote. I grumbled and patted about the sofa, then snagged the damned device from the coffee table in front of me.

I pressed the power button faster than a cowboy could draw his six-gun and stared stupidly at the blank screen until my heart stopped thumping in my chest.

Okay, now this was getting freaky. Or had I somehow stirred in my sleep and nudged the remote with my toe?

"Come on, Anja, get a grip." Too much weirdness was going on around me. Wet footprints, dreams of drowning, and now this? Stress. It must be the stress. Lack of sleep did funny things. For all I knew I could be sleep-walking. My eyes were gummy and I needed to freshen up, so I had that shower I'd promised myself.

I felt better afterward, more alert and rational. After I left a very snarky message on Neill's voicemail, I fixed myself toast with smoked salmon and cream cheese, and spent the rest of Sunday putting the final touches to the presentation.

Fuck Neill, his stupid apartment and my fucking bleeding heart.

Whether the weird shit was a product of my over-tired mind or some bizarre, messed-up paranormal phenomena, I wasn't going to stick around long than absolutely necessary in case I discovered what else this apartment had to offer. I wasn't really afraid – just not in the mood for bullshit.

* * *

Monday morning I managed to get to the office with enough time to make the print-outs for the account executive, somehow get through the presentation without talking the biggest load of kak, then collapse at my desk with the sorry excuse for jet fuel that passed as coffee.

By then I was in a right royal 'don't fuck with me mood' which was the perfect excuse to call Neill's office.

A bored-sounding woman answered.

"Where's Neill? I need to know when he'll be back from his vacation."

"Sorry, ma'am. He's not taken leave far as we know."

"What do you mean he's not booked leave?" I scrubbed at my eyes, smudging my liner.

"We don't know where he is, ma'am. He hasn't come in yet."

This was so not like Neill to just fuck off and not tell anyone where he'd gone.

"Can I help you?" The woman sounded like she'd rather not.

"No." I killed the call without saying goodbye then sat there gazing at a point of nothingness just beyond my desk.

The last ounce of my rational mind screamed at me to go back to Neill's apartment, pack my bag and go home, and just forget about everything. But I had to do the right thing, which was to continue my vigil.

Damn Neill.

He knew me all too well. Once I'd committed to taking on a job, I saw it through to the end. I wanted to kick; I wanted to argue, but right now I was too tired to think straight.

I'd feel better after a solid night's rest. I didn't have any pressing deadlines until next week. One night of vegging out and watching DVDs until my eyes slid shut wouldn't hurt.

I'd try and call Neill's stepmother tomorrow. He must have her number somewhere at home. I'd give him one more day to return my messages.

Somehow I was able to drag myself through what was left of the day then returned to that damned apartment. "No tricks," I said as I locked the door behind me. "No fucking bullshit, okay?"

No one answered me, but that was also fine. I'd have been far more worried if someone had. The fish were happy to see me, and I helped myself to two bottles of Neill's stash of imported Belgian beer which was due payment for the grief.

I promptly passed out on the couch beneath Captain Smith's pompous glare.

Screw the fucker and his brass buttons.

He was dead.

* * *

The air was still, the ocean a pane of obsidian beneath a star-littered sky. I stood aboard the deck of a large ocean liner, one among a throng of hundreds of people who muttered to each, their faces tight with worry while uniformed men winched down lifeboats filled with women and children.

I sucked in a startled breath then exhaled a misty plume into the frosty air. With shaking hands I reached up to touch my face, my skin chilled.

"Please, ma'am, you need to put on your life belt."

I turned to face an earnest young man. "What?"

"Your life belt, ma'am. We've got orders to get the women and children into the life boats."

A ragtime tune drifted gamely into the night. Somewhere a band was playing, and something was wrong - the deck, it tilted so that I had to bend one knee slightly just to feel like I was standing straight, which was difficult in the hobnailed boots I wore.

Wordlessly I allowed the man - who wore a dressing gown over his pajamas - help me into the life belt.

I didn't question him, didn't wonder why I was aboard the Titanic.

I just was.

"Anja!" a man called and I spun to face him even as my helper finished fastening the last strap.

It was Neill, looking dapper in a dark, formal suit complete with fur-lined coat and ivory-topped cane. His face creased in worry, however. "What are you doing here?"

"I-I..." That's when it struck me.

I was dreaming.

"You shouldn't be here," he insisted before enfolding me in a bear hug. He smelled of citrus and cigar smoke, and his breath was warm on my ear.

"What's happening?" I asked.

"The ship's sinking, of course."

I didn't say anything at first, conscious only of my heart hammering like crazy as I gazed up into his eyes. "I shouldn't be here." My lips struggled to form the words.

"No, you shouldn't." He kissed the top of my head then, with me tucked beneath his arm like he always had, he led me to the nearest lifeboat, which was already almost full. "Jackson!" he called out.

One of the stewards turned. "Yes?"

"Please make sure this lady gets a seat."

I grabbed Neill's wrists, the fear twisting through me like a poisoned eel. "What's happening, Neill?"

He smiled at me, his expression serene. "Only what should have happened. Go with the men. You'll be fine." Neill leaned forward and planted another kiss on my forehead, the gesture akin to a benediction, before strong hands pulled me from him and I was helped into the swaying boat.

I was wedged between two elderly matrons, one of whom clutched a Pekingese to her chest. The little dog glared at me with demonic eyes and gave a yap.

Then the boat lurched, and we descended.

Above me Neill stood at the railing, watching as we were lowered. Every time there was a lurch, a few of the women would scream sharply. A child started wailing, inconsolable.

Four stern-faced men manned the oars and the boy at the tiller couldn't have been older than sixteen.

His cheeks were damp.

The boat settled with a splash and soon we were moving from the stricken vessel. All the while Neill watched. I knew he remained at his post even though I soon lost his face in the milling passengers on the deck.

The farther we sliced out, the more pronounced the Titanic's list became. She was lit up like a Christmas tree and reflected on the Atlantic's mirrored surface.

I could do nothing but watch as the inevitable happened. The ship's bow lowered until her propellers rose out of the water.

Exactly like the movie, she eventually snapped in half with the groan of a dying behemoth before the ocean claimed her.

I closed my eyes as the stern was sucked into the unforgiving depths. I wasn't the only one who cried.

* * *

I sat up with a start. My cellphone's display told me it was twenty past two in the morning.

My heart raced and when I swiped at my face, my hands came away wet.

Flashes of the ship cracking in two then slipping below the surface kept replaying, with the accompanying groan of twisted metal.

Shrieks of the survivors bobbing in the lifeboats added a miserable counterpoint. I'm sure that goddamned ragtime band kept playing on board until the bitter end.

"Fuck me." I'd about had enough of Neill's Titanic bullshit. I was going to call his stepmother now, and not a moment later.

To hell with the hour.

I padded to the study, flipped on the switch and scratched around for his phone book.

That's when I looked up at the photograph on the wall. His favorite one, he'd always told me. He'd always drawn comfort from his Rose, as he liked to call the portrait of the unknown woman who'd been photographed as she was about to board at Queenstown.

But it wasn't 'Rose' who gazed down on me from the gilt frame.

It was Neill, grasping the railing, his pose eerily similar to that of the woman though he tipped a hat at the photographer.

He looked *happy*.

It struck me then why the erstwhile 'house-sitter' had looked so familiar.

Rose.

CHOICES IN THE DARK

by Robert W. Walker

The most well-known newsman in all of England, William Stead, sat in the First Class smoking-room aboard Titanic, a cloud of cigar smoke turning his bearded face into a ghostly figure; he'd been caught up in a heated debate with another smoker, one of the most powerful men in America: John Jacob Astor IV.

They debated whether men of power such as Astor owed the world a dime. The two men knew one another well, and Astor, a millionaire, didn't always like Stead's politics or his liberal views; though tonight their friendly banter had taken a new turn, settling in on Stead's recent faith in Spiritualism.

Stead's new venture was a newspaper devoted to the subject, that he called *Borderlands*.

The Spiritualism movement was on the rise, and it was well known that George Bernard Shaw and Sir Arthur Conan Doyle had become devoted members. As a result, Stead had conducted a spiritualist demonstration on board Titanic wherein he was moved to speak from the voice of his spirit guide, a woman he'd met many years before; a spirit now who'd chosen him to communicate from the other world.

Stead's demonstration - a séance - had brought mixed results; he had won over only a few passengers, but he had gained the eye of a certain Mrs. Lorenna Parsons (who was distraught and depressed over the death of her husband, as the poor man had suffered a heart attack and died while travelling across Europe).

Mrs. Parsons had demurely requested a private session to raise her husband as she had not had an opportunity to say goodbye or to profess her love for him one final time.

Stead truly believed that with Mr. George Parsons' corpse in a coffin in the hold below, that his guide, Lenore, could bring Mrs. Parson's husband's soul back long enough for her to say that proper goodbye.

The séance had failed, but Mrs. Parsons still passionately believed in the afterlife, announcing, "I have no regrets at having made the attempt. George, Mr. Parsons, will know that we tried."

Stead had the good heart of a man who wanted to see the world as he dreamed it could be rather than as it was. Mrs. Parsons seemed to have understood this.

Still, there was a practical side to Stead that the world responded to as well; in fact, rumour had it that William Stead was once again being considered as a top candidate for the Nobel Peace Prize for his writings, his service to the notion of 'do unto others as you would have them do unto you'.

He was nothing if not a religious man, strong in the Christian faith and an ardent believer that Satan walked among men on a daily basis.

Stead had originally boarded Titanic for a visit to the USA to take part in a peace congress at the request of the US President, William Howard Taft. Astor was aware of this and also that Stead had lost his wife the year before, that he'd been despondent, and that he had attempted (without luck) to reach her through Spiritualism. They'd had six children, but Astor also knew that Stead did not enjoy the same powerful bond with Lavidia as Astor had always enjoyed with his own wife, Mary Catherine.

"President Taft must be a spiritualist, too, eh, Stead?" John Jacob Astor asked him.

"Scoff all you like, but I've learned a great deal from the practice," countered Stead, his hands busy snipping the tip off his second Cuban cigar of the evening.

"Give me one thing you've learned from the spiritual world," Astor tapped at the ashtray with his own cigar.

"Keep this to yourself, Jacob."

"Of course, if you say so. After all, in the end between gentlemen like ourselves, everything is trust, and the rest is dust."

Stead admired Astor for such pride and character as he always displayed. Astor never failed to surprise him with such succinct truths. "I know now that I will meet my end either by lynching or by drowning."

"And just how do you know this?"

"My spirit guide, *Lenore*. She intimated as much."

Astor knew that Stead had published a story that gained some notoriety twenty-six years earlier in 1886: an article entitled *How the Mail Steamer Went Down In The Mid-Atlantic, By A Survivor*, a semi-fictional piece based on problems he'd unearthed in the shipping industry.

In his story, a steamer collides with another ship, resulting in a high loss of life due to the lack of lifeboats. Stead wrote a moral to his story: This is exactly what might take place especially if liners are continually sent to sea short of boats.

Then in 1892, Stead had published a story called *From the Old World to the New* in which an ocean liner, the Majestic, rescues survivors of a second ship that has collided with an iceberg in the North Atlantic.

"The hangman's noose aside, William, if you truly believe some spirit has warned you to steer clear of water then what the devil are you doing steaming across the Atlantic?" Astor's seventy-year-old grin, along with his cigar, punctuated his remarks.

"I refuse to live in fear, Jacob."

"Then I admire your courage," Astor replied as he watched Stead's expression change from a smile to a look of utter shock. "What is it, Will?"

"You'll have to excuse me, Jacob...I am looking at a...a ghost."

Astor looked over and spotted a heavyset man dressed in a three-piece suit that looked to have been slept in for a week.

The big fellow was rushing through the parlour with two young men at his heels, all three anxious to be somewhere else - or so it appeared.

On or near a train track, the trio would surely be taken for vagabonds. Men of Astor's station and Stead as well, might chalk these three up to Second or even Third Class passengers escaped from below to infest the First Class with their lice.

In their rush, the trio bumped into tables and tripped over one another, but all haste ended when their leader spied the bar. The older man with the bowler hat stopped to order a drink. The two younger men halted too, but they kept nervously and guardedly looking over their shoulders.

Stead sat up, put out his cigar, and stood to excuse himself, leaving Astor to wonder what was going on. Stead sauntered to the ornate bar, and once there, he stared at the man he had thought long dead, and in a shaky voice, he said, "As I live and breathe...Inspector Alastair Ransom? Is it really you?"

Stead's mind raced as he stared at a man who'd been brought up on charges of murdering a priest in Chicago by use of horse pinchers to remove the man's private parts. "How are you are here, on board Titanic? I thought you hung years ago for..."

"It was the useless cleric who molested a boy," countered Ransom, staring into Stead's gray eyes. "Besides, I didn't do it. I only brought the pinching shears."

"The molested child...I recall a street snitch of yours that you were rather fond of, yes?"

"Yes, Charlie, but what does it matter now?"

"Were you acquitted?"

"Fat chance. They had my lawyer murdered!"

"Who?"

"My enemies, of course." Ransom was as big a man as Stead. "My lawyer tried to get you to return to Chicago as a character witness." Ransom slaked his thirst with a second drink.

"It was October...1893. I was in South Africa. I got no such dispatch. Last I heard, you were to be executed."

"Not so loud, Stead, please. Obviously, rumours of my death have been greatly exaggerated."

"Greatly exaggerated, indeed. Here you are!"

"And fancy seeing you here. Hob-knobbing with the rich and powerful nowadays, are you?" Ransom, an aged copper with more interest in his pint than anything else at the moment, was nonetheless intrigued to find a familiar face on board the Titanic. "I'd have thought you shot or hung yourself in some faraway place with a strange-sounding name...Mr. Reporter. That book

I helped you find a publisher for - *If Christ Came to Chicago* caused quite a stir."

"I very nearly was hanged on more than one occasion, yes, but no, I managed to keep my skin. You on the other hand were reported as summarily hung, Alastair!"

"I'll drink to that." He sipped away. "Talk like that keeps me safe. Join me?"

"Who're your young unwashed friends?" enquired the curious newsman.

"Smell a story, do you?" asked Alastair, smirking.

"A reporter's nose still, even at my age, yes."

"I sure as hell have a story for you, Stead. A whopper, really."

"You know me too well, Alastair. Always in search of a good story."

"These two lads are interns out of the university in Belfast."

"Interns? They look the age of the steward turning down my bed tonight."

"They're smart and educated in internal medicine, disease, pathology. They're experts at dissection as well."

"Resurrection men, ha!"

"Autopsiest, sir," shouted one of the young men, having overheard the unkind popular term for men who routinely dissected corpses procured by any means for the medical profession.

"Yes, autopsy men you mean? But aren't you fellows rather young for that line of work?"

Alastair frowned. "They've been vital to a case I am working."

"Ahhh...a case? Are you still doing police work after all this..."

Alastair flashed his shiny tin badge.

"Hold on; not so fast. Let me see that thing!" Stead examined the cheaply made badge. "It's Belfast is it? *Constable* Ransom now?"

"Long story."

"We're on a voyage, Alastair! We've time enough for a story, cribbage, and shuffle board!" Stead laughed at his own remarks before ordering a pint of Guinness to chase a shot of Jameson's Irish whiskey. He then indicated a table in the next parlour. Beneath their feet, they could feel the smooth movement of Titanic over the glassy surface of the North Atlantic.

It was a perfect night, the heavens filled with stars, and the air had a bit of chill clinging to it.

It was April 14, 1912 and Stead's watch read 9:11PM.

Ransom left his two young friends at the bar, having indicated that he wished to speak to Stead alone.

A moment later, he and Stead were seated across from one another and having a close-quarter staring match, sizing one another up. After a while, they reminisced about a time during the Chicago World's Fair when Stead had published his now infamous book: *If Christ Came to Chicago.* "I still owe you a great deal, Alastair," he admitted.

"Bullswallop that!" Alastair changed the subject by lifting his pint. "Good Irish beer this! Could dim the lights in here a bit, they could."

Stead refused to be diverted. "We both know I couldn't have done that book without your help. You got me around that wicked city of yours when I was a bungling neophyte there."

Ransom waved this off even knowing Stead was right. He had enlisted Ransom's help in uncovering the worst of Chicago's underbelly, and Ransom had come through for him, making his book better for it. Alastair said now, "You're well-respected, Stead, and I imagine you've been seated at Captain Smith's table a time or two."

"Well as a matter-of-fact, just last evening we discussed what pleasant weath..."

"Perhaps Smith will listen to you then!" Ransom voice rose as he cut his old friend off. "The damn fool refuses to listen to me, the boys there, or to pay heed to the photographic evidence. He's without reason."

"Reason?"

"He won't listen to the experts - the two young doctors, Declan Irvin and Thomas Coogan - on a matter of life and death."

"What bloody matter of life and death are you referring to?"

"The lives of every man, woman, and child on board this ship - potentially."

"Potentially?" Stead parroted the word.

"And exponentially those of every man, woman, and child in New York as well," added one of the young interns who introduced himself as

Declan Irvin. The pair of boy-doctors in Ransom's company had seated themselves at a table close enough, it appeared, to better eavesdrop.

The second intern called himself Thom and shook Stead's hand, telling him he'd read many of his dispatches over the years. He then qualified the other boy genius' words with, "If this ship docks as if nothing were amiss, sir, it will be like turning a horrible contagion on the most populace city in America."

"What sort of strange business have you gotten yourself into, Alastair Ransom?"

"The captain refuses to listen to our story," added Declan, holding tight to a journal with a leather tie holding it together.

Thom Coogan, blinking with sleepiness said, "They threw us into the brig instead. Dogs and cats howling all night."

Stead stared at Alastair and burst out laughing. "Captain Smith had you thrown into jail? Below-deck? Ha! I still haven't a clue how you escaped a Chicago jail, and now you're arrested aboard Titanic?"

"The lot of us, aye," muttered Ransom, "'cause your captain is a fool!"

"He's in fact a quite intelligent, well-read old gent on this, his last voyage, and he likely took you for..."

"The competition, I know; I realize that. He thought the big wigs of the Cunard Cruise-line put us up to the whole thing, but Stead, it's all, unfortunately, true about there being a contagion aboard here, and the ship needs to be quarantined. You've got to talk to the man on our behalf."

"I've not seen you in years, you escape the hangman's noose in Chicago, now sporting a Belfast badge, and you come to me with this wild story?"

"I realize it's been a long time, Stead. Look, I wound up in Belfast where we..." he indicated his young accomplices, "...we first discovered this, *ahhh,* problem on board here."

"You're going to have to convince me, Alastair, that there's a real threat." The newsman's nose twitched while, beneath his full moustache, his beard was bobbing. He sensed he was onto a good story.

"You have to believe us. It's...well, it's a disease that's widespread aboard this ship, Stead."

"A disease, so you've said? Gone rampant, has it? Widespread, you say? Look about you. I see no evidence of any such problem."

"Not here, no, not in First Class, but the lower deck infirmaries are filling up rapidly," lied Ransom.

"*Ahhh*, I see...from the scourges in Third Class, eh?"

"Yes, yes, a real killer, it is."

"Which is it, Constable, a disease or a killer?"

"Both," declared Declan.

"Below in steerage, eh...would figure that Captain Smith would want to keep it hush-hush." Stead stroked his beard, a sure sign he was buying into the idea, or at least partially so.

Ransom jumped on Stead's deduction and continued to lie. "Yes and it's making its way up to First Class, William. You could be a hero in this matter, you could...if only..."

"*Hmmm*...go on. Tell me more."

Ransom told Stead the entire story of how two miners had contracted the disease first. "Both dead after working the mine that provided the steel plating on Titanic and her sister ships in the Belfast shipyards."

"Then came my uncle's death," said Thomas, a tear in his eye.

"Your uncle?" asked Stead.

"Antone Fiore...was the shipyard watchman," added Declan. "And a good man, he was."

"Then it was one of the private detectives, a fellow named Tuttle..." began Ransom.

"Private detective?"

"A hired gun to guard Titanic."

"Against what, against whom?"

"Against any possible anarchist plot before she should set sail for Southampton, William."

"The men who were taken by the contagions, sir, they all died excruciating deaths," Thom added in an attempt to return the conversation to the moment.

Declan said, "The autopsy photos will show you that their bodies had been turned into incubation chambers."

"Incubation chambers?" Stead remained incredulous.

"This disease, this thing...it takes over a man's body and deposits eggs..." insisted Ransom, "...sac-like eggs that hatch inside a man and feeds on his entrails until there's nothing left, William."

"This sounds impossible, like some Bram Stoker novel, a penny-dreadful; no wonder the captain locked you up."

"He took the advice of the ship's doctor; a closed-minded, practical man; nothing like you, William."

"We even showed them photographs of the things," said Declan.

"Like I said, they thought we were working for some rival ocean liner!" Ransom said incredulously with a half-laugh. "Damn fools. Can you talk to Smith, Stead? Make him see reason?"

"Where're the photographs you say you have? I'll have a look at them."

"With your knowledge of photography, yes, you could authenticate the shots."

"Let me see these autopsy stills."

"I'm afraid Captain Smith has 'em; if he hasn't destroyed them by now."

"I'll take a look at the photos, and I'll talk to Captain Smith. You can trust me for it, Alastair. But tell me, how is it transmitted, this disease you're talking about?"

"You believe in Satan, Stead. I know you do."

"I do indeed. You forget, my father was a minister."

"I'll let young Declan here explain it to you."

Declan cleared his throat and said, "The disease is transmitted from person to person; this thing behind it takes over a man's body, using it as an incubator; when the seeded eggs hatch, they make a meal of the host body, thoroughly devouring it for survival."

"That sounds perfectly draconian, but there are precedents in nature all around us of such parasitic creatures."

"See, boys?" Ransom said to his young associates. "An open, well-read mind and someone who is well respected. We merely need to petition the captain once more."

"But how does it first get into the human host?" asked Stead, ignoring Ransom's aside to his friends.

"It has a mysterious capacity to leap into a new host body. I mean at this very moment, it could be alive inside me, or Declan or Thomas." Both boys laughed as Ransom shrugged, "Hell...could even be in you...or it might even be in our Captain Smith!"

"How then can you know it when you see it coming?"

"That is our greatest problem. You can't know it and you can't see it; but one thing is certain."

"What's that?" Stead leaned in to catch Ransom's near whisper.

"The demonic...it may take a pleasant shape; just know so from your Bible and your life experience. Stead, old friend, this ship needs to be quarantined. Since departing Southampton, we've been trying our damndest to convince Smith of this!"

"You've been in the brig all this time?"

"Most of the voyage so far, yes. We'd hoped to stop the ship...it's why we boarded, me and the young doctors-to-be here."

"May Jesus save us if it's true!"

"Uh-oh....gotta go!" Ransom saw two burly crewmen with Mr. Murdoch, the second lieutenant coming through from the other end of the smoking parlour.

Murdoch had armed himself in the hunt for Ransom and the other two escapees. Alastair saw that his young friends had also noticed the commotion, so the threesome bolted to find a safe place to hide from those who wished to imprison them again.

Stead sat statue-like as Constable Ransom and his two friends rushed out one end of the parlour while young Lt. Murdoch, his pistol half-hidden via a neckerchief, rushed after them.

The men with Murdoch eyeballed the bar, slowing enough to tell Stead that they'd much rather be having a drink than chasing Ransom up and down ladders and lifts. While others in the smoking and drinking parlour appeared oblivious to the action going on around them, Stead's trained eye caught it all.

Then Stead's gaze met Astor's and he knew the sharp old tycoon knew something was amiss as well. A third person, a finely dressed lady in white, had also taken in every nuance of the excitement down to Stead having had a conversation with Ransom.

Up until tonight, the only dress and veil Stead had seen this lady wear was her black mourning clothing. 'A Certain Mrs. Parsons', the other ladies aboard called her.

She had boarded in Southampton in black garb and had remained so until now. Her husband, George Parsons lay in a coffin along with many another body crossing the Atlantic to be buried back home in the States. Stead had fancied the tall, slender, beautiful Mrs. Parsons before but more so now.

Stead looked at his watch to see that it was now 10:11PM.

He thought it odd that Mrs. Parsons was out at such an hour, as ladies, even on a cruise such as this, typically took to their rooms before dark, excusing themselves with remarks of 'beauty sleep'.

Stead motioned her over to his table, and out the side of his eye, noticed that Mrs. Astor was also up, but it was quite clear she had come to fetch Jacob and lead him off to bed. Stead admired the amazing bond between the Astors, the unconditional love they had for one another.

He had never known such a love, despite all his years of marriage. Now it seemed something powerful within him had been stirred up by Mrs. Parsons who just happened to be half his age.

Stead knew it was hopeless entertaining the thoughts of a foolish old man as after all, he would soon be sixty-three. He'd not looked at another woman since his wife had passed the year before.

He'd not one scintilla of a thought of a woman of any substance or worth ever finding him worthy of her affections, yet Mrs. Parsons seemed attracted to him for some reason beyond his reckoning.

She'd gravitated to him since the second night of the voyage. They had shared the rail one night, had shared a stroll on deck, had sat at his table, had given up a smile for him, and now this.

He even dared to imagine that she'd come straight from her bed to find him here.

For days now on the cruise, they had enjoyed one another's banter; she had proven a worthy and well-informed adversary on various issues.

Like most educated women, she had been sceptical of the efficacy of Spiritualism, or that he could indeed make contact with her deceased husband, but something about her made him so want to help her in her time of grief, and to possibly win her over.

He'd gone some distance even before the séance to convince her that it was a faith in keeping with all charitable Christian beliefs.

He'd pointed out instances of 'spirits' found in the Bible. He spoke of Jesus' own spirit rising from the dead, and of Lazarus before him.

"Mr. Stead." Mrs. Lorenna Parsons offered her gloved hand, and Stead quickly stood, took it, kissed her hand through the cloth; helped her to a seat at his table.

She smiled at him, her eyes hidden below her white veil. "I suspect my being here in your company so late will be the talk of the ship by dawn."

"My lady, anyone who dares say an unkind word about you will have me to deal with me. Would you care for a glass of wine? Brandy perhaps? To help you sleep?"

"I would prefer some water only."

He nodded and rushed off to fill her order.

Lorenna made him feel like a schoolboy, and he felt the need to put a bit of distance between them even if for a moment. Then he saw the way Jacob Astor and certain other old men in the room looked at him when he was in Mrs. Parson's company.

They must be thinking the same: that he was acting like a love-struck old fool. Else the more vulgar among them were giving vent to their own fantasy involving the widow. By the time he reached the bar, Stead decided he didn't care a whit as he lifted a pitcher of water and a glass, and returned to Lorenna.

"You needn't wait on me, a man of your stature, Mr. Stead."

"I thought we agreed you'd call me Will? As to fetching you water, it's rather late, and the number of stewards is down to the poor fellow behind the bar."

Stead silently played her name over in his mind and tried to imagine what his life might have been had he met her twenty years before, and then he realized how foolish the thought, for she'd have been a mere child then. Their eyes met. She sipped at her water, he at his ale. She reached across and took his hand in hers. "I don't want to be alone tonight," she said in a low-toned, whiskey voice.

"Neither do I," he admitted in a whisper.

"Then why are you here alone, and I alone in my stateroom?"

Stead swallowed hard. He could not have imagined these words coming from the grieving widow, but he realized she must be so very lonely on this ship with over two thousand strangers on board.

She was vulnerable and as she said, *alone.*

He quibbled internally with himself for being a fool even as he did his best to convince her she was not acting in her own best interest. "Perhaps you really just need someone to talk to, and perhaps we should stroll along the promenade. Others on deck are star-gazing, I'm sure."

"Here...take this, and please come." She placed her stateroom key in his hand, and as Stead stared at it, she added, "I will be waiting, William."

He watched her as she glided like an angel, her beautiful white dress whispering as it swished against the empty tables and through the doorway.

***

Stead now had two requests from two totally unexpected avenues: one, to speak to Captain Edward Smith regarding the photos left with him to determine their authenticity, to investigate like a reporter the amazing allegations of a disease-spreading demon aboard Titanic...and now this second request: one from a beautiful young woman to join her for companionship in her stateroom.

Stead squeezed the key in the palm when he felt a hand on his shoulder. He looked up to see that it was old Jacob Astor - his wife at the opposite end of the parlour, a kind, patient smile on her aged face that seemed a match for her husband's smile.

Two of the most gracious people he had ever known, and they both knew what was going through his mind. Or at least one half of his mind.

"Why are you still here, Jacob?" Stead asked the old tycoon.

"Live it up for me, tonight, William. Go see the lady. You have every reason." Astor indicated the key in Stead's possession.

"Join your wife, old friend, and have a pleasant night yourself, and *stop* worrying about me."

Astor slapped him on the back, still a strong man even at his age. He laughed as he returned to his wife, and Stead realized only now how empty the smoking parlour had become.

Only a few remained along with the band playing in the ballroom adjacent, sounding as if they were practicing new tunes, new routines.

Closer to hand, a rowdy bunch of poker players in one corner appeared to have had one too many drinks as well as hands played.

Stead got to his feet. If he followed the route the Astors had taken, he'd go directly to the bridge and locate Captain Smith, look into this strange and unusual nonsense that Ransom had laid at his doorstep, but if he exited the door that Lorenna Parsons had gone through, he'd follow his heart.

He thought of the old saying: 'the heart wants what the heart wants' and his heart wanted to find her in her stateroom where he would take her in his arms, comfort her, even if for a single night.

Just suppose, his fevered mind asked...what if this choice - this night - led to the kind of bond that his friends the Astors had enjoyed for so many years?

Glancing at the poker players, he could just as well take a third option. Join in and take them for all they were worth. Instead, he saw the futility of wealth as never before, and instead, he asked himself if there might not be a ghost of a chance that he and Lorenna could find lasting true love and that ephemeral thing called happiness?

What he found initially, was himself helplessly walking through the door where he'd last seen Lorenna.

He'd deal with Ransom's curious story and Captain Smith and the so-called autopsy photos tomorrow.

When he got to Stateroom A-48, Stead felt good about his decision. He had a genuine smile on his face when Lorenna opened the door the moment she heard the key in the lock. She was dressed in her robe, already anticipating Stead's coming to her.

Just as he had imagined, he took her in his arms and kicked the door closed. They embraced in the darkness, modesty still in the room with them. He gently cast off her robe and felt his way about her body, his fingertips quivering, her skin responding with a growing fire.

She kissed him passionately, and he responded by deepening the kiss, then by moving his hungry mouth over her at every curve, crevice, and juncture. She led him to the stateroom bed, and there they began the dance of love that Shakespeare once called the *beast with two backs.*

Stead's mind reeled with her touch against his skin when he began to feel something else crawling along his skin, something not normal, something supernatural.

He lay in bed, paralyzed, when he suddenly recalled Ransom's warning: *The demonic may take a pleasant form.*

As if in a dream or a narcotic state, Stead realized that he had fallen prey to the demonic thing - perhaps Satan himself - aboard Titanic.

His last curiosity was his wonderment as to precisely when Mrs. Parsons had first become a carrier. Was it that first night she'd approached him? His deflated ego, he knew, was the least of his worries now.

He watched her rise above him as if floating and recalled how she'd glided across the parlour room, and he realized she was not a corporeal being.

She had also stamped her will onto his as if an infusion of a strange, inky mixture like an evil octopus had injected him, and in its impact on his senses it had reduced him to her zombie.

His brain and limbs belonged to her; he knew too that whatever she wanted, he'd have to give over to her now. In fact, he could not recall even having thought of ever having a will of his own.

***

11:11PM saw the great ship Titanic rend herself on the spur of an enormous iceberg.

After the ship struck the iceberg, Stead helped several women and children into the lifeboats, among them 'A Certain Mrs. Parsons'.

This report from Henry Fleet was given over to the New York inquiry board into the cause of the horrible disaster that claimed over one and a half thousand lives.

Fleet, the first man to have spotted the iceberg from the crow's nest added. "I never seen such a brave man as was Mr. Stead, except maybe both Mr. and Mrs. Astor. The old girl, she wouldn't leave her husband's side."

"As for Mr. Stead's actions…everyone said it was typical of his generosity, courage, and humanity, how he insisted on getting that poor widow onto a lifeboat. You know, after all the boats had gone, Stead went into the First Class Smoking Room, where I last seen 'im sitting in a leather chair and lookin' over some photographs, he was, but the look on his face...well he was lookin' like a man without a single care."

A later sighting of Stead, by survivor Philip Mock, had Stead clinging to a raft alongside John Jacob Astor IV who'd leapt into the frigid water holding hands with his misses, but she never surfaced. Astor grabbed onto the upturned boat and kept saying to Stead: "You shoulda got on the lifeboat with the widow." He called Stead a damn fool.

"I made my choice," was all Stead said.

"We didn't have much in the way of choice, did we, Will?" Astor replied.

Mock then told the inquiry board, "Their feet and lower extremities were frozen, you know, and they had no choice. There in the dark, they released their hold on the raft - an overturned collapsible lifeboat is what it actually was. Both men, both fine gents, drowned before me eyes, they did, and nothing no one could do about it."

William Stead's body was never recovered. Further tragedy was added by the widely held belief that he was due to be awarded the Nobel Peace Prize that same year.

Among the Titanic survivors was a certain Mrs. Lorenna Parsons who refused to give a single interview to hungry reporters, all save one who mysteriously disappeared.

She also refused to speak at the New York and London inquiries into what brought the ship down.

She was distraught as she had been engaged, after all, in transporting her husband's body across the Atlantic for burial at home in Upstate New York - a corpse now at the bottom of the ocean.

Sadly, she arrived in New York Harbour aboard The Carpathia, the rescue ship, having lost any and all opportunity for a proper burial of her husband.

Those few who were close to the veiled Mrs. Parsons - very much in black again - got the distinct impression she did not honestly care that her husband's remains had disappeared with Titanic as she spoke more highly of William Stead and how marvellous Spiritualism was than she ever spoke of her husband, George Parsons.

Mrs. Parsons soon sold off all of her husband's land holdings and relocated from the rural farmland of Upstate New York and into the city where she took a modest apartment.

Not long after this relocation, a disease began to decimate entire portions of the city, primarily among the poor and infested shanty districts. Death became a daily part of life in the 'city that never sleeps'.

One disease in particular was so pernicious and cruel that all autopsies were kept secret so as not to alarm the general public about strange and alien egg-sacs growing in their loved ones' corpses...

THE JASPER SCARAB

by D.T. Griffith

Henry Burgess leaned over the countertop to inspect the brooch.

"A survivor you say," said the Central Park South antiques dealer on the corner of Eighth Avenue, as he positioned the nearby swivel arm lamp for better illumination of the scarab's soft details. "I didn't know that about you. Impressive."

He balanced the jewelry delicately across his outstretched fingers to study the glyphs inscribed on the reverse. "Come to think of it, you are only the second survivor I've ever heard of."

"Yes, my mother wasn't so lucky, died that night in the freezing water. I try not to talk about it much."

"God bless her soul..."

"I shouldn't be here," William said staring at his shoes. "I wanted to go down with the ship as the men were supposed to do. But I was thirteen, not quite a man in the eyes of those who placed me in that overcrowded lifeboat."

"I'm sorry, Willy. I would have never guessed."

William stepped back from the dented oak counter and assessed his surroundings. "Same overcrowded boat my mother fell from...it was such a long time ago."

"Oh dear. Surely you don't blame yourself?"

William did not respond.

"I can only imagine the horror."

"It took over twenty hours to recover her body. This brooch was still on her necklace."

The two men stood quietly, both staring at the counter.

Burgess broke the silence. "This brooch then," he held up the green scarab set on a pair of gold wings enameled with dark colors, "how did you come across such an intriguing piece? This stone appears to be jasper. Authentic."

"I spent my childhood in London. About a year before the Titanic voyage," he paused to swallow his rising anxiety, "or should I say catastrophe. Anyway, I attended a mummy unwrapping party with my mother."

"Really? I've heard wondrous things about such events."

"Not all that exciting when you realize it's just a dead guy under those filthy rags stuffed to the gills with dried flowers and putrid mud."

William noticed an Egyptian-styled bust sitting on a shelf behind the dealer's counter. "Items like that," he pointed at the small sculpted head, "would make the long journey back from the tombs along with the mummies to the grand homes of London's social elite."

"This scarab is an ancient Egyptian piece, I have no doubt about that. But the brooch setting... I would say it is about fifty years old, the style was popular back then."

"All this time I thought I was a carrying around an ancient artifact. I took it from the unwrapping party. Everyone was so marveled by the dead guy they couldn't bother with a simple beetle shaped piece of jewelry and other shiny trinkets."

"You were a naughty boy Willy; this was a fine lady's piece of jewelry." He chuckled as he adjusted his glasses. "But the scarab in the middle: that's your artifact. And it's jasper, not too many of these floating around."

William placed both hands on the edge of the counter and leaned in toward Mr. Burgess. "Well, it's yours if you name a good price."

The dealer inspected the tiny ringlets welded on the backside of the gold wings adjacent to the exposed scarab's underside. "These aren't original."

"My mother had a silversmith in London add them so she could wear it on a necklace for the Titanic's maiden voyage. It was my birthday gift to her in February that year."

"I see." He held a magnifying glass over the scarab's green body; near-perfect linear carvings defined the insect's body segments. "I will pay you one hundred fifty dollars. And a discount off your next purchase here."

"Sold."

William accepted the cash from the antiques dealer, shook hands, and left the store.

"Dammit, looks like snow again," he said walking through the crowded sidewalk at Columbus Circle to his third storey walk-up just a block away.

Free from that devilish thing at last, he thought, picturing Janna Lee, his first fiancée three years prior. She wore the brooch on the night of their engagement dinner only hours before her deadly automobile accident.

A freak coincidence? He wondered often. Of course. No piece of jewelry, no matter how old, could cause such things to interfere with the lives of real, wholesome people.

But then there was Olivia, his Greek goddess, as he liked to call her, whose parents immigrated when she was two years old.

Ahh, Olivia.

Her large brown eyes and black curled hair, an evocative dream of a woman.

Until that damned tuberculosis robbed the world of her beauty and kindness three months after their engagement. He remembered her sweet gesture: she wore the brooch to honor the memory of his mother to a wedding the night before William offered his hand.

Perhaps there was a connection to the brooch.

A tear fell across his cheek, he let it resonate a moment before wiping it away with his kerchief carefully situated in his breast pocket.

Three women he loved, gone from this world because of that evil thing. Meanwhile, he managed to survive it all – a catastrophe at sea, an auto wreck, and a disease.

William arrived at the foyer of his small apartment building. "Good day, sir," said a tanned woman descending the stairs.

"Good afternoon, miss. Are you the new tenant on the second floor?"

"Yes," She held out her hand to shake his. "Octavia Clemens."

"Nice to meet you, Miss Clemens. William Boyd."

"A pleasure, Mister Boyd...I must be on my way. I sure hope we meet again soon. Enjoy the afternoon."

"Good day," William called after her as she hurried out the door.

An exotic woman had he ever seen one. Mediterranean skin with blue eyes. "Incredibly beautiful," he whispered and smiled as he walked up the three flights of stairs to his home.

* * *

The wail of sirens woke him.

"Six after three," he groaned reading his alarm clock, "you kidding me?" William rose from his bed, wrapped a robe around his cold body and peered out a street-facing window. "Dear god! A fire!"

He could see the firefighters on the street with pumper trucks and a hook and ladder truck, trying to temper the flames the next block down.

"Looks like Mister Burgess's building...this can't be happening," he said, rushing to pull on his trousers, boots, and his wool overcoat.

He ran down the stairs, missing a few steps at a time, stumbling and catching the rail as he reached the bottom flight, and charged out the door to the street.

"No no no!"

A crowd of people had already formed on the street around the brownstone that housed the antique shop; some aiding the firefighters with blankets and water for the residents rescued from above the store.

"Where's Mister Burgess," William shouted. "I need to see Mister Burgess!"

"He didn't make it," a man in a black scallycap said.

"What are you talking about?"

"He came running out to the street already on fire, collapsed in the snow. I suppose he was hoping it would douse the fire. Poor guy."

William shrieked. "How does this keep happening?"

"Probably arson, mister, or maybe a short with his electrical..."

"No you don't understand, I'm responsible," William cried and ran toward the burning storefront. There he found Burgess's badly burned body, stiff in the snow under a woolen blanket.

"This isn't right." He knelt next to Burgess's body to whisper a prayer.

"Step back, sir," a tall police officer said. "This is an active crime-scene."

"I knew this man."

"You must step back for your safety."

William noticed a sparkling reflection of the fire near Burgess's hand. He leaned in closer for a better look.

The scarab.

He yanked the brooch from Burgess's firm grasp and pocketed it before the policeman would notice.

"Thank you officer, I understand," William said as he retreated from the scene.

"I saw that," a woman shouted from the crowd, surrounded by other people who were comforting her.

He turned to see Mrs. Burgess glaring at him. "I'm so sorry about your husband, he was a good man. I will say a prayer for him tonight." He hurried away.

William returned to his home gripping the scarab in his coat pocket, running his thumb over its intricate details. "I can't take this anymore," he said softly as he climbed the stairs. "I need to lock this away so no one can find it."

"Can't take what?"

William turned to see Miss Clemens peering through the door he had just passed.

"Sorry... I didn't mean to disturb you."

"Nonsense," she said, "I saw that fire too. What a frightening night."

"Frightening indeed." William smiled. "Let me make this up to you, lunch is on me tomorrow. Does noon work?"

"You are the pursuant type Mister Boyd, I'll give you that. Noon it is."

They said their goodnights, and William ascended the stairs one slow step at a time. "What am I to do this with this cursed thing?" He considered throwing it in the Hudson, but someone could always find it washed ashore down at beaches in Brooklyn.

Too risky, he wagered...it needed to be a place that only he knew about, that only he would ever have access to and no one could find without his knowing.

The floorboards of his bedroom closet were loose in a corner...

William tore off his coat and flung it on his tufted leather reading chair, shipped from his family's estate in London when all was settled after his mother's death.

No returning to London, he felt, not another sea voyage ever again.

New York was his home now, one for which he grew quite fond.

He opened the creaking door to his closet. "Need to grease these bloody hinges," he muttered as he knelt on the uneven floor.

Images of Burgess's corpse flashed in his mind, as he felt around for the loosest section of the floor in the near dark.

"Why was he holding this thing?" By surprise, William removed a length of flat oak with ease revealing the perfect hiding place.

He reached for a simple wooden box on the shelf next to the closet he kept buttons in and emptied the contents onto the floor.

He placed the scarab brooch inside the box, fastened the buckle lock and placed it softly in the hiding place.

"You have taken too many lives. Never again. This stops now."

With that he pressed the board back into place and whacked it a few times with his palms.

It still felt loose, but he was confident no one would come across it without his knowing...

* * *

Three months passed.

William and Octavia had decided to dine at the recently opened Rainbow Room.

"A most beautiful view," she told William, peering over Rockefeller Center. "The ice skaters below, the golden statues, the lights. The Empire State Building right over there. A city girl's dream."

"I'm happy that this place brings you pleasure, my dear sweet Ava," he cupped her right hand between his, gently raising it to his lips. "Your happiness means the world to me."

Octavia laughed, "William, since when did you start calling me Ava? And speaking with this silly properness?"

"Just a cute nickname. I hear it in your name, Oct-Avia."

"I suppose you're right. Then I'm Ava to you, Willy."

The couple laughed together and finished their dinner.

"Ava, what is that on your necklace? May I have a closer look?"

"Oh, yes, I found this in a wooden box back at the apartment."

William leaned over the table for a better view; Octavia removed her scarf to reveal the full piece of jewelry.

Its polished surface gleaming in the low restaurant lighting, the dark colored enamels appeared to glow in the warm illumination of the candlelit table.

"The scarab. How did you find that?"

"It was in a little wooden box on the floor of the bedroom closet." She studied William's face. "It's like somewhere left it there for me to find. Why? Is there something wrong?"

"This was my mother's...when I was a child."

"It is beautiful, William," she gently lifted the brooch off of her skin and rested in on her palm.

It dangled from a newly attached silver chain. "You know my mother's family came here from Cairo," she said, rubbing the surface of the brooch with her thumb then repositioned it at the center of her neckline. "Simply beautiful."

"It is," William said with some hesitation. He wanted to tell her of the brooch's dark history, but no words formed as he tried. He had planned to ask for hand before seeing the brooch, but decided it was best to wait.

After dinner, they exited the building for a walk in the early spring air. "It's finally warming up," said Octavia, as she looped her arm with William's. "I can't wait for summertime on the shore," she announced. "I found the most beautiful bathing suit last week." They walked north on Sixth Avenue toward Central Park.

"I enjoy this time of night," William said, "so quiet, no traffic, almost no one around."

"It is a wonderful night," she confirmed.

William pondered his next words carefully. "That scarab brooch you are wearing, it's beautiful, I agree, but it has a bad history."

"It's just an object...."

"I mean, people who had once worn it, or held it, are no longer with us."

"But that's normal with antiques," she mused.

Without warning, William felt a hard edge against his throat.

"Don't you move, or your girlfriend's brain takes a spill."

A dark figure appeared from an alleyway, most of the person's face concealed...William realized it was a woman.

She glided toward Octavia, pointing a small pistol at her head, and lifted the scarab brooch hanging from her neck, studying it in the streetlight. William could not see his assailant behind him except for his outstretched leather-clad hand.

"Your wallet and your watch, now," said the voice at his ear.

"I don't have much," William spoke softly, keeping his fear in check.

He dug his hand into the inside flap of his jacket. He felt the round bevel of the small pocketknife he carried next to his nearly exhausted money clip, carefully unfolding the blade with the edge of his thumb.

"Your money and watch, I said." His attacker's sharp blade pressed further into the tender skin just above his larynx. He imagined warm blood trickling down the front of his starched shirt, the embarrassing sight that would be.

With the pocketknife securely gripped in his palm, money clip held between his extended fingers, he slowly removed the contents from his jacket.

"This is all I have," said William, passing the cash into his left hand, keeping the small knife palmed in his right.

"Your watch…take it off and hand it to the missus." The assailant snatched the money from William's hand.

"Don't worry," Octavia whispered. "It's just a watch." William saw the pistol press lightly against her forehead.

William slid the golden expandable band from his wrist, hooking two fingers in a tight grasp around the band, the blade positioned slightly outward.

Octavia choked on her words as she maintained her composure. "Do as he says, William, please."

The female assailant lunged the barrel of her gun into Octavia's mouth. "Shut your trap, bitch, if you know what's good for ya." She yanked the silver chain breaking the clasp; Octavia emitted a grunt. "I'm taking this back."

"Gimme the watch," the man demanded, his left hand held out in front of William's face again.

William brought his own hand toward his attacker, dropping the watch before the exchange could be made.

"Son of a bitch," the attacker grumbled. "Don't bloody move."

William felt the pressure of the blade on his neck diminish as he heard the assailant crouch to search for the watch on the sidewalk.

He spotted the gloved hand come close to the watch and kicked it away, stomped down on the hand and swung his right arm around planting the pocketknife in the side of the man's neck.

The masked man shrieked and toppled backwards grasping at his wound. His partner watched, fear visible in her eyes.

Octavia seized the moment and grabbed the pistol with both hands, forcing the barrel under her attacker's jaw.

She noticed the brooch dangling from the woman's hand and tried to snatch it back.

William grabbed the woman's arms from behind to restrain her while watching the masked man writhe on the sidewalk, blood spraying from the wound in his neck.

"Ava, give me the gun then run for help, I'll stay here and hold her." Octavia reached toward William with the gun over the woman's shoulder. The woman's forehead butted against Octavia's wrist with enough force to drop the pistol.

She kicked back at William to free herself and punched Octavia in the abdomen, forcing her to double over, and smashed her knee into Octavia's face.

William regained his stance and reached for the gun, the woman elbowed him in the face and grabbed it.

"This is for my Henry," she shouted and pulled the trigger aiming toward Octavia's head. The scarab dangled from the masked woman's hand, the polished surfaces contrasting with her all-black clothing.

But, the trigger jammed.

"Ava, run!"

Octavia rolled away from the masked man's blood pooling around her and stood up. Her footing was unstable; her nose a mangled mess.

The woman continued to yank on the trigger aiming at Octavia.

William quickly grabbed the back of the woman's head. With all of his weight he forced it down flat on the sidewalk in a single motion and repeatedly smashed her face into the concrete until she stopped resisting.

He slowly regained his composure and knelt next to Octavia.

She had collapsed while he took out the female assailant. He leaned in and kissed her lips softly and clasped her hands.

"My head...I need the hospital," Octavia whispered. William helped her up. They looked at the two piles of twisted and bleeding bodies lying on the dark sidewalk.

"I want to see their faces; then we'll go to the hospital." He leaned over to pull the knit mask from the man's face: no-one he had ever seen before.

Then he pulled off the woman's and stumbled back.

"Anna Burgess," he said, "widow of the antique shop owner." He began to cry. "This doesn't make any sense."

"William, please I need to go…now."

He spotted the scarab brooch clenched in Anna Burgess's hand, the broken silver chain strewn on the pavement, and speckled in blood.

As he reached for it the brooch tumbled out of her hand and landed next to his foot. He pocketed the jewelry piece, located his money clip and wristwatch, and escorted Octavia back toward Fifth Avenue to find a ride to the hospital.

"Survived again," he said rubbing his thumb over the scarab's carvings remembering his mother's blue and bloated face as he pushed the brooch deeper into his pocket...

THE BRINY DEEP

by Kyle Rader

They had met in passing; purely a chance encounter. Both had taken a fancy for a stroll around the open decks of the great ship and, as the massive steel and metal monster crested a large swell, Ms. Amesbury lost her balance and fell into Beauregard's arms.

Conversation ensued, starting with the embarrassed, awkward pleasantries one feels necessary after committing a social faux pas. It quickly moved to more pleasant topics: Beauregard's reason for taking the maiden voyage (he was a professor of history, off to the States for a lecture tour), whether Ms. Amesbury traveled alone (she did and she wasn't afraid in the least), and how they each felt about the great miracle of the modern age they sat upon.

"Kind of feels odd," Beauregard remarked.

"What does?" Ms. Amesbury said.

"This is an achievement that shall never be rivaled in our lifetime. I'm used to teaching history, not being part of it."

Ms. Amesbury laughed. Her giggles: waifish and not those a woman of her age, nor prestige, should make coated over a subtle mockery enough that Beauregard did not notice. "Oh, Mr. Beauregard. You are rather silly, aren't you? Every day you live, you are becoming a part of history. Sometimes the little things and the little people matter just as much as the paramount."

A kiss on his stubbly cheek stifled any further thoughts on the subject. "You act as if a lady has never shown you the slightest bit of kindness." Ms. Amesbury said.

"Yes. I...I mean, no! I...I mean..."

"It is no matter. We shall be friends, you and I, for as long as this vessel carries us across the Atlantic. Oh! Look at the hour! I've got an appointment in the Massage Room. Do excuse my abrupt leaving, Mr. Beauregard. We shall see each other shortly. Yes, tonight, in fact! Tell me, have you heard whispers of the private parties held by the Captain?"

"Everyone has. I didn't give them much thought. A man of my traveling class stands a better chance of being swept overboard than to receive an invitation."

"It just so happens that yours truly has been invited to tonight's event, a very, *very* special one, or so I am told. You shall come as my escort, Mr. Beauregard, I insist."

Ms. Amesbury had a pleasant enough face, but, there was something about her that had Beauregard on edge. He couldn't place it, couldn't even determine if his fears were something even tangible at all.

Later that evening, Beauregard found himself on the arm of Ms. Amesbury. She led him through sections of the ship of whose luxury was the stuff of dreams. Portholes covered in Arabic curtains made to appear as if they grew from the walls. The dying light of the day shone through the veneer, giving the rooms and corridors the very color of the Orient, mysterious and exotic. They walked upon carpeting that cost more than Beauregard made in a year and through a series of dizzying twists and turns before stopping.

"Take heart, Mr. Beauregard. We are here!" Ms. Amesbury stood aside and, with one hand on her hip, gestured to a small door. Unlike its contemporaries, with intricate carvings of clocks, sea creatures and the like, this door appeared more at home in a basement. Its only distinguishing features were a heavy iron knocker and an image scrawled into the wood.

It resembled someone's idea of what a large fish should look like. The head was bulbous and made up the majority of its body, while the tail was forked into jagged triangles. Standing out was the large oval eye of the beast. A faint red stained the splinters, as if someone had considered painting it, then changed their mind upon the first dab.

"What is that there? Some kind of symbol?" Beauregard asked.

"This? Oh, this is just some graffiti one of the old salties put up. Superstitious lot, they are."

"It's rather hideous, isn't it?"

"Pay it no mind, Mr. Beauregard. Even palaces made of gold and silver have nooks and crannies that shine a bit less bright than the rest. Now, what say you accompany this proper lady to this proper party?"

Ms. Amesbury smiled without emotion as Beauregard slipped his arm around her and knocked on the door. A short man in a white tuxedo and red cummerbund greeted them. "Ah! Ms. Amesbury! We've been expecting you," he said with a glossy-eyed stare and a smile filled with teeth too small. "And, this must be your guest, Mr. Beauregard! A pleasure, sir. Do come in, and might I add that you look resplendent in that gown, Ms. Amesbury."

"Oh, Joe, flattery will get you *every*where."

Joe stood aside as the couple walked into the room; billows of smoke escaped into the corridor. Beauregard felt the man's eyes upon him the entire time. He did not like the man, but said nothing as not to upset his hosts nor Ms. Amesbury. What he found most troubling was not the leering, but what lay upon the man's waist: a silver pin in the very shape of the symbol etched upon the door.

***

Despite his misgivings about Joe, Beauregard stood in total agreement with the man on one thing: Ms. Amesbury did look radiant in her gown. Azure in color, it billowed down her body as if poured upon her by of one of the Greek gods. A ribbon of forest green tied into her hair and a pendant that hung low into her bosom elevated her to paradigms of beauty otherwise unobtainable.

Beauregard's awe was fleeting, for his thoughts turned inward and deprecating. The people gliding around the room were the chosen ones; perfect bodies and wealthy beyond design, whereas he, the son of a failed poet, was life's cruel joke. He did his utmost to keep his shirt tucked into pants two sizes too small and kept his arms clasped behind his back as to mask the series of tears in his suit coat.

Ms. Amesbury disappeared amongst the crowd the second she waltzed Beauregard through the door, leaving him to slink off to the nearest corner. There were many people; much more than he'd thought could fit into such a small room. Sweat coated him from the combination of body heat and the roaring fireplace. *Whose idea was it to light a damn fire in here?*

"Hello there, Old Bean. Are you not our guest, Mr. Beauregard?"

Beauregard, lost in his world of self-conscious hell, almost failed to hear the words coming from the stranger. Looking up from the hole he was staring into the floor, Beauregard found the man standing so close, their noses brushed against each other.

"Y...yes," Beauregard said as he took a step backwards, only to find the oak boiserie holding him captive. "Yes, I am he. Who might you be, sir?"

The stranger's laughter rippled down Beauregard's spine with the same subtle mockery Ms. Amesbury tried so hard to conceal. "Are you feeling quite well, man? Your color does look a bit off. Surely that can be the only possible explanation for failing to recognize one's host, the very Captain of the R.M.S. Titanic, E.J. Smith!"

Beauregard's cheeks reddened to even darker shades than the heat of the room had already turned them.

What a fool you've made of yourself, he thought as Captain Smith, wearing his full regalia nonetheless, explained his error to the party. The crowd laughed at him. Their faces blurred into one; a monster made of melting flesh and disdain.

"We are just having a bit of a go at your expense. All in good fun." Captain Smith placed a hand on Beauregard's shoulder. It was not a reassuring gesture, rather somewhat menacing. The old sailor had much vigor in him, proving this by pressing down on Beauregard hard enough for him to hear his collarbone creak.

"Yes, Mr. Beauregard. Take no offense at the Captain. His sense of humor is normally as vibrant as his beard, but perhaps he has been at sea too long." Ms. Amesbury emerged from the crowd, sashaying through the miniscule space between the bodies to stand before Beauregard; a drink in one hand and the other behind her back.

"Quite so. I would not dream of offending you, sir." Captain Smith shook Beauregard like an earthquake, sending his lower jaw crashing into his upper.

"Quite all right," Beauregard said. His eyes sought the door. His feet shuffled his body in the direction he believed it to be only to be returned to his starting point by Captain Smith; the man's grip seemed to be made of the same wondrous metal of the Titanic itself. "I...I do rather believe that I should retire for the evening. I've got a lot of notes to organize for my lectures and I dare not risk falling behind."

All ambient noise of the party, the clinking of glasses, the pouring of libations, the small talk and laughter, vanished. The focus shifted towards Beauregard, and only Beauregard. Every man and woman stared at him with the same wild-eyed expression that Joe the porter had.

"I'm afraid that is simply impossible, Old Bean."

"Yes. The guest of honor cannot *leave* his own party. Certainly not before receiving all of his well-wishers. It simply will not do." Ms. Amesbury sipped from her glass. The deep red wine stained her mouth, coating her teeth in runny crimson.

Captain Smith pulled Beauregard forward; the crowd parted without prompting. "I do believe that it is time, my friends. Our dear guest seems rather eager to be canonized. Who are we to deny him this great honor?"

"Canonized? What the devil are you speaking of, man? Let go of me at once!" Beauregard shouted over the appreciative roars of the crowd. Struggling against the Captain's clutches proved futile, so he changed tactics and went on the offensive. He kicked at the man's legs, screaming as his first, and only, successful attack ricocheted off the Captain's shin. Beauregard felt the bones snap and crumble in a dozen places. He fell, only to be hoisted up by the indomitable strength of Captain Smith.

"Easy now. You've just got a case of the nerves. It'll pass once we begin the ceremony." Ms.

Amesbury whispered to Beauregard as he was dragged to a couch; his shoes hovered an inch off the floor.

He was set down with the utmost care. Captain Smith ensured that he had a pillow under his head and his injured foot. Something caught Beauregard's eye as the man stooped over him. Upon the Captain's lapel was a medal that was an exact replica of the hideous giant fish upon the door.

My God, they're everywhere! The portrait of the Leviathan surfaced all around him. It was carved into the wooden paneling, sculpted into the mantel of the marble fireplace, even the pillows he rested upon had the creature embroidered into the fabric. Beauregard yelled for help until the inside of his throat was torn into strips.

"There, there, Mr. Beauregard. Save your strength for the ceremony. You don't want to stand before the face of God without a voice in which to praise him, do you?" Ms. Amesbury smiled down on him in the manner that a farmer would a horse with a broken leg. She rose and nodded to Captain Smith, who returned the gesture and stood upon a table.

"Friends, the long promised hour is upon us." Reaching into his suit coat, Captain Smith produced a mask and placed it over his face; the partygoers followed suit until all were wearing the symbol of the great fish. Bone white, the masks reached down past the nose and had but a single eye, the same vile, all-seeing one from the effigies.

Beauregard struggled to sit up, but found two sets of hands holding him on the couch. *What lunacy was this?*

"Here, Mr. Beauregard, I brought an extra." Ms. Amesbury slipped the mask on him. It was cold, freezing in fact; the interior formed a suction cup to the skin of his face. The room grew more sinister from the craggy oval he viewed it from. Leviathans affixed to dozens of faces bombarded him; the wearers of the masks grinned wider as they regarded him in some sort of awe.

"From the time of our fathers and their fathers before them, we've worshipped in secret, in backrooms and closets away from 'decent' society, the usurpers having driven us there with their Inquisitions and heretical lies," the masks rose in unison; their owners screamed for justice and howled for the blood of their enemies until Captain Smith calmed them. "Yes, my friends. I share your pain, having borne it for so many years. They called our beliefs barbaric! They called our Lord pagan filth! Nothing more than a trick; an agent of their great and powerful Satan, a *being* - I might add - of *their own creation!*"

Cries of "Damn them!" and "Kill the Deceivers" interrupted the Captain, whom did not seem to mind, as evidenced by the yellow-toothed grin frozen upon his face. A majority of the ire found itself re-routed to Beauregard. The worshippers of moved in a slow circle around him. Insults barked out from underneath the tail of their masks. Malice bled from their solitary eyes, making the great fish appear even more predatory.

Ms. Amesbury emerged from the circle of hatred and sat beside him, resting her head upon his chest. The intimacy of the embrace felt obscene to Beauregard, making his blood boil with anger. "This all just part of the ceremony you silly man. No need to get so upset. All of these people revere you and are eternally grateful for your presence."

Captain Smith waved his hands over his head; the followers grew silent instantaneously. "For centuries the Order of the Briny Deep has watched the world, watched and waited, waited for the prophesized time to arrive. It pleases me to no end that I can tell you - with the utmost certainty - that tonight our long wait is finally over!

"Years have I watched for the signs of our Lord's coming, seeing a multitude come to pass - the ritualistic slayings in Whitechapel; the assassination of an Archduke, leading to a great fall in the world. Yet, the most telling sign of all is the very vessel in which we find ourselves now. This, Titanic, the marvel of the modern age, is the final key to unlocking our Lord's return to the realm of man. From its very conception, we've had agents placed at every level, from the engineers down to the porters who dust the lampshades. It is to be the crown jewel in *our* Lord's crown, not that of any government of man. None of this could be possible without the tremendous efforts of our High Priestess, Ms. Amesbury; her considerable wealth and influence exhausted in the service of our Lord."

Ms. Amesbury nodded to the Captain, who motioned to two followers, who placed a whalebone basin on the table before him. The symbol of the Great Fish had been carved into the rim and along the sides. "What is that supposed to be for?" The disquiet in Beauregard's voice rose as Ms. Amesbury left his side to join Captain Smith. "*Tell me what that is!*"

"My friends," Captain Smith said. "Our Lord drifts towards this vessel in his icy tomb. Shortly, he will be freed from his long tormented slumber, free to dole out judgment upon the world and drown it with his might. The passengers of this 'Titanic' will serve as worthy sacrifices. Their souls - which will be hurled screaming into his maw - shall provide him the power necessary to break free.

"As we know from the holy tomes, this is all for naught unless we purify this place - and ourselves - so that it and we may be welcomed into our Lord's eternal service. Ms. Amesbury, the blade if you please."

The knife was rudimentary, little more than another hunk of whale bone fastened to a scrap of driftwood. Yet, its presence exhibited an air of respect upon all who looked at it. Taking it in his hand, Captain Smith raised it to the sky, then to the symbol of the Order behind him. "In your service, Lord of the Briny Deep, your humblest of servants, do sanctify this vessel and all whom travel within it with the blood of the innocent."

Ms. Amesbury leapt from Captain Smith's side and straddled Beauregard. "That's your cue, Mr. Beauregard." She tore at his suit coat, not stopping until her nails left behind frenzied trails that flushed with his blood.

"Get off me, you crazy woman!" Beauregard managed to knock Ms. Amesbury onto the floor, only to receive a punch to the temple for his efforts. More hands held him firm, pinning his exposed arm to the armrest of the couch. He saw multiple knives cutting him, slicing a straight line from his elbow to wrist. Blood pooled in his palm fast, arousing tremendous panic within him.

The sound of his life striking the bottom of the whalebone basin was that of a sopping mop hitting a floor. Beauregard wept as it filled.

And then, he was released; tossed back against the couch, forgotten. Cradling the dire wound to his chest, Beauregard flung his mask aside and scuttled off the couch, falling upon the floor. A weakness claimed him, pulling him face-first to the ground. He felt cold. Sleep prodded him, sitting on his eyelids to keep them shut. Sluggish, he pulled his way past the legs of the worshippers, now seeming not to care one whit about him. A corner behind the altar served for a resting place and a chance for him to get his bearings. "Oh, God."

The Order stood with their hands raised to the sky, then pointed towards the symbol of their Lord; their fingers itching the empty space, desiring to possess it. Beauregard's ill-gotten blood drenched them to the wrist. Stray droplets plummeted onto their masks, dying them a muted pink.

"Children of The Briny Deep," Captain Smith's voice boomed. "Will you help to prepare our Lord's transition back to the world that cast him out?" The cult replied with guttural shouts of ascent. Captain Smith looked to Ms. Amesbury and smiled. "Having bathed in the blood of an innocent, I beseech thee, one and all, let the Culling commence.

"Ms. Amesbury, if you would do the honors?" She stood before Captain Smith; whalebone blade in hand. Without any sign of ill-intent, the woman plunged it into the Captain's stomach, pressing it in up to the hilt. Bubbles of blood exited the man's mouth, each living only for a moment before the bristles of his beard destroyed them. The Captain looked towards his flock one last time and then collapsed onto his back, never to rise again.

Ms. Amesbury twisted the knife, yanking it free. "The course of the ship is set. We shall meet our Lord in less than ten minutes time. Hurry now, lest you find your soul being devoured for all eternity instead of riding on our Lord's fins."

With those honeyed words, the slaughter began. Cultists grabbed the nearest person, man or woman, to them and attacked. Beauregard watched in horror as he saw knives disappear into stomachs and necks, as hands turned white from squeezing the breath out of throats. One woman produced a Derringer pistol and blew her brains out of the top of her head. All of the deceased and soon-to-be deceased smiled, *smiled* in unadulterated joy. This chilled Beauregard to his very marrow.

Acrid blood hung in the air. Beauregard retched. He dared not close his eyes for fear that one of the Order would slice him apart as part of their demented ritual.

His back found an unlocked door leading down one deck; faded paint on the inner wall pointed down towards the Bridge. *Got to get out of here and warn someone,* he thought. *There's got to be someone in charge who hasn't lost their mind.* He stood on legs that felt like another's and shuffled down the spiral stairway. His feet moved of their own accord, skipping steps and turning in odd angles. His vision grew narrow, blurred. *Must hurry. Cannot let them crash the ship. All those people,* he thought, squeezing his bleeding arm to his chest tighter.

The Bridge lay before him. A simple room filled with machines that Beauregard would need years to study to figure out what each did. They were of no consequence to him, for he knew exactly which piece of equipment he sought.

The wheel lay not on the Bridge proper, but in a small windowed room behind it. The door held firm when Beauregard attempted to open it. Undaunted, he summoned his fleeting strength and smashed into the metal frame with his full weight; the door did not even shiver. He tried again, then again until a loud pop resonated and his arm fell lifeless to his side.

"Goddamnit!" He pressed his face against the large window of the wheel-room; his hard breathing steamed the sleek surface. Through the fog, Beauregard saw the reason why his efforts had failed. Two officers lay dead on the floor, their hands coated in Beauregard's blood and with canyons carved into their throats. One of the dead had, rather ingeniously, wedged the door shut with a piece of steel rebar.

"Pointless to resist, Mr. Beauregard."

Ms. Amesbury leaned in the open doorway of the Bridge; the cool sea air blew in from behind. Her dress, once beautiful, was now ruined, covered in the blood of at least a dozen men and women. "The wheelhouse, locked. The wireless room - if you could even get there in time - destroyed. Even those flares to my right that you're eyeballing have had their powder removed. Nothing has been left to chance. This is our night. Our Lord shall return. Who are you, little man, to stand in the way of a God?"

Beauregard grew faint. He steadied himself on the corner of a cabinet. Ms. Amesbury moved close to him in the time between the drops of his heavy eyelids, appearing as the smiling, demure woman who engaged him in polite conversation and then as a blood-crazy murderess clutching a pearl handled knife standing directly in front of him.

Blood assaulted the metallic floor, dripping from blade and Beauregard both. It took great energy, all that he had left, but Beauregard looked into the eyes of his killer and said: "You poor, poor fool. Your corpse will choke the waters along with the rest of us. Your faith, your *Lord*? They are naught but lies."

"Well, Mr. Beauregard," Ms. Amesbury placed her gloved hand against his cheek; the blood of her Order left behind a crimson streak. "Just a few minutes more and we shall see, shan't we?"

A smile, one last gleeful, cruel smile and then Ms. Amesbury opened her own throat. Arterial spray covered Beauregard, blinding him. Gagging, he wiped his eyes clear on his sleeve. Ms. Amesbury lay upon the floor in a state of serenity; eyes closed.

The night sky was clear for an April. The moon and stars reflected upon the choppy waters of the Atlantic, providing just enough light to see the iceberg directly ahead, the final doom of the Titanic; the so-called Lord of the Briny Deep, come to regain its place amongst the world. It encompassed the entire horizon, as if it had swallowed the globe, leaving nothing but it, and only it, as the supreme ruler.

Before the last life trickled down Beauregard's arm, he looked upon the iceberg.

For a moment the iceberg looked back.

LE LABORATOIRE DES HALLUCINATIONS

by Dean M. Drinkel

15th April 1912, 5.32AM

The air and the ocean were still, like glass.

There were sounds. Agonising cries.

But they seemed so far away.

Suffocated by the darknes.

Unreachable; echoes perhaps...confusing.

One small boat cut through the water like a shark's fin.

Daley stood at the bow shining the lantern before them; Drew sat with the oars in his hands, rowing as slowly and as carefully as possible (but trying to keep warm all the same) and at the stern Black; binoculars to his eyes, ascertaining what was real, what was flotsam and jetsam – he didn't have a lamp but did the best he could.

They had been out there for several hours, dispatched from the Carpathia to search for survivors, even though everyone knew the odds were stacked against them. A few lucky ones had been rescued but that was hours ago now. Other boats had returned to the Carpathia empty-handed, but these three men decided to carry out one final sweep, just in case. That was their duty.

There had been rumours that there were lifeboats full of survivors just waiting for someone to guide them to safety but if that was true, these men hadn't seen them.

There were also rumours that there were plenty of survivors too *in* the water, clinging to each other for succour, for dear life, but if there were...

Yes, they had found of plenty of bodies, corpses, cadavers, that was true – but survivors, not.

Hope was running on empty and Drew was going to complain that his arms smarted and though he didn't want to admit defeat, he knew that would be that if things continued the way they were going.

Suddenly Black made a noise in the back of his throat and he asked Daley to shine the lantern port-side; illumination was needed urgently.

"What did you see?" Drew asked.

"I'm not sure...over there...look!"

Daley tried his best to shine the light where his friend pointed. "I can't...I don't think there's anyone there...I'm sorry..."

"I'm telling you...it wasn't my imagination...come on man get closer..."

With great difficulty, Drew managed to get the small boat moving again, heading in the direction where Black motioned.

Daley shone the lantern in a complete circle.

Nobody spoke. The only sound was their breathing.

"I know what I saw, I know what I saw," Black panted.

Daley did another sweep with his lantern. "I'm sorry old man but if you did, they've gone now." He paused. "I don't want to be a killjoy but let's call it a night, we tried our..." He stopped then shifted slightly, the boat creaked as he did. He wasn't a light man.

"Careful, careful, you'll tip us over into the drink," Drew warned.

"Did you see something too?" Black asked, his voice dripping in anticipation.

"I'm not...yes, yes, over there, look!" He waved madly.

Black squinted through his binoculars. "I knew I was right." He dropped them onto his chest.

It was true. There was something, someone, floating in the water.

"We need to be swift," Daley called. "They look done for...they're being pulled under..."

"I'm trying, I'm trying," Drew exclaimed, moving his right oar.

When they were as close as they dared, they saw that it was indeed a man, a young man, his body...

"Why isn't he wearing any clothes?" Black asked. "That's a tad unusual isn't it?"

"Can you tell me one thing about this night which is usual?" Daley curtly replied, then smiled, he hadn't meant to be so short.

"Let's get him out of the water, he must be freezing," Drew stated. "Let's pray he's not dead already."

Daley put down the lantern, got to his knees and then leant over the side. "Christ, its cold. Help me will you?"

"Of course." Black moved past Drew (who tutted under his breath as he was having problems keeping the boat upright and steady with all this moving of body weight).

The two men reached into the depths. "He's going under again!" Daley shouted. "Hurry, or we will lose him!"

"Not if I can help it," Black replied.

As much as it pained them, they managed to grab the young man and pull him into the boat.

Daley blew into his hands, was that frostbite already? The water had been like ice. He rubbed them on his trousers, not that that made much difference.

Black took the lantern, illuminating their passenger.

"My goodness, he's almost completely blue. Is he alive? What in God's name has happened to him?"

"Look at the state of those wounds," Drew stated. "I'm sorry; I think we may have had a wasted journey my friends."

The oarsman's statement regarding the appearance of the young man was painfully correct: a nasty gash to his head; one eye was badly bruised, so much so that it had fused shut; numerous wounds to his wrists, his ankles, around the genitals.

There were also what looked like deep burns to his stomach, his thighs; one nipple sliced clean away. His hair was in patchy burnt clumps; all over his body were small fresh scars which looked like...medical stitches?

Daley leant down, frowned; then smiled. He removed his coat, then using it, started to rub the young man's flesh. "He's alive, I could feel his breath...there's a feint pulse. Come on, the quicker we can get back to the Carpathia then we will have more chance of saving him."

"Okay, okay." Drew sighed as it took him a couple of strokes to get the boat moving at a steady but rapid pace.

Black took off his own jacket and helped Daley to dry the young man off and keep him, hopefully, in the land of the living.

"Hello! What's that?" He held the young man's right hand, it was clenched tight, like a claw...there was something inside. "It's a small piece of wood."

"It must have broken off whatever he held onto to try and keep himself afloat," Daley suggested.

Black moved the lantern. "Perhaps from a door or something?"

Drew scowled as he rowed; his arms were killing him, he needed to get back as soon as he possibly could, get himself in front of a stove to warm up...a nice mug of tea. "Why do you say that?"

Very carefully, Black opened the young man's fingers, careful not to snap them, and retrieved the object. He held it in the light so the others could see it too.

A number '16' was engraved upon it, in brass.

"Wait a minute, do you hear that?" Daley asked. "He's trying to say something."

He leant down. "What was that son? You're going to be okay...we've got you now...we're taking you to the Carpathia."

The three men remained as silent as their chattering teeth would allow.

Suddenly the young man's one good eye sprung open, such terror imprinted there on his retina, his face scrunched up in a ball of pain.

"Papper!" he screamed. "PAPPER!"

His body arched, he kicked out but then his chest collapsed, his head lolled to one side.

"Damn it, has he expired?" Black asked.

Daley rested a hand on the man's neck, felt around. "There is a pulse...its weak...come on let's get back...let's not lose this one..."

He grabbed the young man's hand and squeezed it as hard as he could. There had been too much death these past few hours, he wasn't going to be responsible for another one.

***

Traveler's Aid Society, New York, June 1st 1912

Doctor Oldham entered the makeshift ward; he flipped through the charts on his clipboard.

A red-headed nurse stood by one of the beds, he didn't recognise her, though that wasn't anything out of the ordinary – staff had been coming and going on a regular basis in all the chaos.

She wiped the sweat from the brow of a young man. The sheets and blanket were pulled up close, right under his chin. He was barely awake, pallid; terribly grey; his face bruised.

The doctor smiled, tapped the clipboard with the end of his pencil.

"He's lucky to be alive, Nurse...?"

She hesitated for a moment then (was that his imagination?) looked down at the name-badge on her uniform. "Purvis," she said eventually and without much conviction.

"Purvis," he repeated, breathing in. Was that cigarette smoke he could smell? If it was then standards certainly were slipping. He would have to have a word with Matron when he had finished his rounds.

"What happened to me?" the young man whispered. His eyelids heavy; a frown skipped along his forehead.

"How much do you remember?" Doctor Oldham wrote something down.

"I was on a ship," he explained.

The doctor nodded, sat down on the edge of the bed. "That's right: Titanic. It wasn't indestructible after all, it seems. Hit an iceberg. There were...you're one of the lucky ones."

"I don't feel lucky...can I have something to drink?"

The nurse picked up a small glass, filled it from a jug of water, put it to his parched lips – he drunk heartily, so much so that some spilled down his cheeks, onto the pillow. She grabbed a cloth, wiped up as much as she could.

"Everything hurts," the young man said eventually.

"I'm not surprised. You've had a rough time."

"Yes. Think hard, what do you remember about that night?" the nurse enquired.

Again that frown. "Nothing's clear...it hurts so much..."

Doctor Oldham glared at the nurse, yes, he would certainly have to speak to Matron – what training were these girls getting? There was something odd too about her face: it was stony, sounds were coming out of her mouth but the tongue seemed too big, the lips too...something didn't seem right, but he shook his head, he was so tired...

"There's no need to force things just now, take your time, you need your rest. Perhaps in a couple of days, when you've recovered some more, we can try and figure all this out." The doctor turned, walked away, headed to the next bed.

"Forgive him," the nurse whispered, out of earshot. She rung out the cloth in the small bowl. "He means well, he's a good man, just sometimes his bedside manner isn't what it should be."

The young man smiled. "He is American."

"Yes, I suppose so." For a moment she seemed distracted. She rubbed her jaw, he heard it click.

"But you're not...I don't recognise the accent...sorry."

She rested the cloth on his brow. "I'm Irish mainly, I guess. Dublin. I've been here a while, I pick up accents quickly. A natural mimic my father used to say. You wouldn't believe me if I told you a month or so ago I spoke with an Austrian accent." She laughed at her own statement then shook her head. "Pay no attention, my mouth can run away at times." She looked at her hands, as if for a moment she was surprised they were on the end of her arms.

"There was an Irish girl on the ship," he paused. "I seem to remember that."

"I suspect there was plenty. Pretty was she?"

"I don't recall." He coughed. "My body is killing me."

"The doctor was right, you really are lucky to be alive, if those men hadn't found you when they did..." She fought back the tears.

"Is there anything you can give me? I'm in agony."

"I could do but I don't want you relying on that...you need to keep away from the chemicals, from the drugs. You don't know what you've had in your system."

"What do you mean?"

"You just need to be careful that's all, we don't want you overdosing do we?"

She went over to the window, stared out.

"What time is it?" he asked.

"Almost midnight." There was a full moon.

"How long have I been here?"

She paused for several moments. “A few weeks.”

“Weeks? My god...”

She turned back to him. “Don’t fret yourself about that for now. Concentrate on getting better. We need you fit and healthy.” The nurse went to the end of the bed. “Can you remember what your name is? Or anyone we need to let know you are here? A wife...or sister perhaps?”

“Richardson. Yeah...James Richardson. That sounds right.”

“Good, good.” She was beaming.

“A reporter,” he stated. “At least I think I am. Was.”

“You were writing about the Titanic?”

“I guess so.”

“You’re not sure?” She sat down in her chair.

“No.” He stared at her. “Have we met before? There is something familiar about you...I don’t know what it is...sorry is it me, I can smell burning, can you?”

The nurse looked away.

“I didn’t mean to embarrass you. I’m sorry if I’ve said the wrong thing.”

She turned back, touched his face. “I’m not embarrassed, quite the contrary.”

“Do you have any tea? I’ve suddenly got a craving for it. It might put my mind off this...agony.”

“Some sugary tea could do you the world of good. Early Grey was your favourite...” She stood up, went to the door.

Richardson didn't respond to her statement, there was something else on his mind obviously: "That girl."

"Girl?"

"On the ship. The Irish girl."

"What about her?"

"She was killed. He killed her."

"He? Who is he?"

His eyes closed. "I don't remember. My mind...its dark...I don't know...I'm confused."

"We don't need to worry about that for now...leave it to the police...they will probably want to speak to you now that you are awake."

"Did they find her body? There's something..."

"Let's have that tea, get some sleep, gather your thoughts, then tomorrow, in the morning, we can speak some more. I know someone who will be interested in what you've got to say."

"I am feeling tired."

"I won't be long."

***

Nurse Purvis closed the door behind her. Her shoes clicked on the polished floor. With no-one watching her she went into the office at the far end of the corridor. She sat down at the desk, opened a drawer, and took out a piece of paper. She picked up the phone, dialled a number.

"Yes?" a voice eventually answered. German.

"He's here. The reporter."

A slight pause. "Say that again."

"He's here. In the hospital. He's alive."

Another pause. "You are positive it is him?"

"Of course I am! He doesn't remember much, only bits and pieces at the moment. Do you think...?"

"We will have to make sure it stays that way."

"What?" Pure panic in her voice. "Surely you don't mean after everything..."

"I will speak to Doctor Papper. Contact will resume at six o'clock tomorrow morning. Make sure you pick up."

She drummed her fingers on the desk. "Doctor Papper? But I thought..."

"You heard me. Six o'clock."

The line went dead. She dropped the phone down in its cradle.

She was crying.

Not tears of sadness, but of joy.

Doctor Papper.

He was alive.

***

"...Doctor Ernst Papper."

Richardson leant down, grabbed the old man's hand. For someone so aged and with obvious disabilities, the grip was strong...

"Over there Gustav, by the window."

"Of course Herr Doctor."

Richardson stepped to one side as Papper was pushed across the wooden floor. His manservant straightened the blanket then took two paces back.

"Half an hour. That should be sufficient," Papper instructed.

Gustav bowed and departed.

"I do not bite. Come closer." Papper signalled to Richardson who joined him, sitting down in an empty chair. "That's more like it, don't you agree, just the two of us - we can talk, like old friends?"

Richardson nodded.

"Accept my humble apologies that we didn't meet at the earlier allotted hour. It was not my intention to renege on our agreement but I was not feeling myself, I'm sure you understand. Travelling vast distances can play havoc with my constitution..."

"Think nothing of it."

"Even so," Doctor Papper coughed into his gloved hand.

"We could go back inside if you wish?"

"I'm fine, really I am. In my dim and distant past, there was a fire. It seems so long ago now but had terrible repercussions. I'm fortunate to still be here."

"Vienna wasn't it? I seem to remember reading..." Richardson smiled.

Doctor Papper's eyes narrowed. "Correct." He took several deep breaths; let the gentle breeze caress his face. "Your telegram wasn't clear...something important to talk to me about wasn't it?"

"That's right," Richardson muttered as a man, a woman and a small child walked along the deck. “Did you hear about that girl who has gone missing? Vanished into thin air apparently.”

Papper leant back in his wheelchair. “And you think that has something to do with me? Are you the police? You think that somehow I am involved. It would be interesting to hear your hypothesis.”

Richardson held up his hands. “Of course not! That came out all wrong. That’s not at all what I want to talk to you about…but back in the saloon, while I was waiting I heard someone mention that a girl had gone missing and…”

“What was her name?”

“Pardon?”

“This vanished girl. What is her name?”

“Oh right, yes.” He searched his pockets, found a crumpled piece of paper. “Wilson. Joanna Wilson. Irish apparently. From somewhere called…Wexford?”

“Was she attractive?”

“I don’t know, I never met her.”

“There are many pretty girls on this voyage…” he pulled out a small silver bell from under his blanket, he gave it a gentle shake.

From seemingly out of nowhere, Gustav approached, bowed. “Herr Doctor?”

“At dinner two nights ago, there was a young girl sitting with us at the Captain’s table. Dark red hair. Irish possibly. According to this young man she has disappeared.”

Gustav stared menacingly at Richardson. “Is that so?”

"Speak to the Captain. Offer our assistance. Everything must be done to find her."

"As you wish."

Richardson watched as the manservant left.

"Efficient isn't he?"

Doctor Papper smiled, titled his head slightly. "Very."

A few moments awkward silence followed until Papper picked up the mantle. "But as you said, you didn't wish to speak about the girl."

Richardson shook his head, took out a notepad and pencil. "I am interested in you, Doctor Papper. It is very rare for you to come out of Paris where you now reside...since the fire you mentioned..."

Papper nodded his head solemnly. "I do not talk about my private life."

"...so when I heard you were to be aboard Titanic, I didn't want to miss the opportunity."

"But why am I so important to you and your newspaper of which I know the proprietor by the way..."

"The whole world is interested in you."

Papper chuckled. "Now you are appealing to my vanity."

"I don't mean to." Richardson wetted his lips. "An eminent doctor such as yourself? People come to you, you don't go to them."

The smile remained.

"And here you are; a vacation to the Americas?"

"Precisely. A vacation, nothing more...I think you've misunderstood my purpose."

Richardson frowned. "I don't think so...I've heard..."

Papper shifted his weight. "What have you heard?"

"That you are on the way to the Americas to visit a certain Doctor Dupin, an expert in what the populace is now labelling 'plastic surgery' but you would perhaps call facial reconstruction..."

Papper stared at the young man for several moments before bursting into laughter. "Plastic surgery...why would that be of interest to me? There was a certain Madame Tussaud..." He punched the side of his wheelchair. "As you can see my injuries are little more than..."

"Not for you," Richardson started, almost smugly.

"No?"

The reporter shook his head. "No...for your children."

Papper appeared to lose his composure. "I don't have any children. Check your sources, I could almost be offended."

The young man scratched his forehead, unconsciously labouring his point. "I understood you had a son and a daughter, twins...Emile and Solange?"

"I have just said: I have no children."

"Yes but...

"If Doctor Papper says he has no children, then he has no children."

Richardson turned, Gustav stood there. "Apologies...you are needed."

"Wait a moment, your telegram reply stated I would have half an hour...I didn't mean any offence...please, Doctor Papper..."

No further words were uttered as Gustav grabbed the back of the wheelchair and began to push the doctor away. Richardson flicked through his notebook, searched through the clippings, pulled out a small tattered photograph.

"But if you don't have any children, then who are these? Phantoms?" He called.

"Get out of the way!" Gustav warned.

"I implore you Doctor Papper! Who are two children in this photograph? I'll tell you what I believe...they are your children Doctor Papper...Emile and Solange. They were in a terrible fire, they were burnt beyond recognition but somehow they lived, God knows how but they did...they are now either in Vienna or Paris...you're keeping them alive and you need the help of this Doctor Dupin to..."

Richardson tried to force the photograph under Papper's nose but he turned away disinterested.

"I'm not going to tell you again," Gustav stated steely.

Eventually Richardson backed away, his hands up in mock surrender.

Gustav glared at him as he pushed Doctor Papper along the deck towards the prow of the ship.

Richardson, shaking, headed in the other direction, back inside the saloon.

He needed a drink.

A stiff one.

***

The saloon was busy.

Richardson ordered himself another whiskey; found a semi-quiet area and sat down. He sipped at his drink, took out his notebook and began to jot down some words, sentences, phrases. He was onto something, it was just a question of what exactly.

"Do you mind if I join you?"

He looked up. It was a woman, no more than a slip of a girl actually. Attractive, well, thinking about it, he guessed she was attractive, though he couldn't see too much of her. What with the arm-length gloves, the headscarf, the hat, the small sun-glasses which were de rigueur in certain low-land countries. What he could see of her face, the skin was pale, but not offensive...a pretty little nose, strands of bright auburn hair evident.

She held a glass of champagne. "This your first voyage?" she asked, a hint of an accent, though he wasn't exactly sure of where it originated – it was definitely European.

"Be my guest." He pushed out the chair for her. She sat down.

"Do I know you? There is something vaguely familiar..." He had definitely seen her somewhere before...but the way she moved, it was almost as if her body was foreign to her…an awkward gait…

"We've never actually met…though I'm an admirer of your work." Her cheeks dimpled, blushed slightly.

"Really?"

The girl shrugged. "I've recently spent some time in London...your prose is second to none."

"I'm flattered, madam."

She leant out, touched his hand lightly. "You should be…it's not often that I pay compliments."

He raised his glass. "Then I thank you very much."

"Santé," the girl replied.

Richardson left it a couple of moments before asking. "So who exactly are you and where do you come from? Is there any more like you at home?"

She leant back, seemingly in contemplation. "That is a very long story. I could tell you but I doubt you would ever believe me." They stared at one another, he wasn't sure whether to take her completely seriously and when she burst into giggles and the tension released, he laughed too.

"I am in need of a cigarette…do you partake?"

He shook his head. "I'm sorry, I don't; I could never take to it."

She eyed him curiously but then shrugged. "I have my own tobacco."

The girl stood up, he followed; taking her arm they strolled outside, under the awning, by the railing. She looked skywards. "I prayed we were to see some stars tonight. God lets me down. Often," she mused.

"It is very cloudy. A storm is heading our way"

She shivered. "Almost a portent..."

"A portent of what exactly?"

No answer. She rolled herself a cigarette (very expertly!) which she lit, taking several deep inhalations. She sipped from the champagne, leant over the railing. "I love the sound of tidal water."

"I haven't really given it much thought."

Flicking her cigarette into the air, she quickly grabbed him, pulled him into her. "Then for once listen man, listen. Can't you hear that? Doesn't it scream at you that you are alive?!"

A man and woman walked by, they nodded to him when he caught their attention, he smiled weakly.

"Um...another drink?" Richardson asked.

She put a finger on his lips. "You do talk a lot don't you?"

"That's what I'm paid for..."

He felt that the way she stared at him was awkward, contrived. He stared into her eyes, really stared into them. They were so bright, so blue. But it was as if there was something else...something else there hidden. Another soul hiding away back there.

It took him a couple of moments to realise that she had started talking again. Suddenly she stopped.

"I was miles away...I didn't mean to be rude. What was that?"

She put a hand on her chest, feigned that she was hurt, upset. "I asked you whether you knew anything about the girl that went missing. Everyone's talking about it."

He couldn't stop looking into those eyes; it was as if he was in a dream. He shook his head to clear it. "Missing? Yes, I did actually." He wondered why so much of her flesh was covered; he imagined removing it layer by layer...

"She was Irish, so I heard..." Her words brought him out of the daydream. The way her lips curled when she had said Irish, he wasn't positive she was being pleasant.

"Apparently she was very very pretty," Richardson replied absentmindedly.

"You saw her then?"

Richardson didn't answer, he was distracted. His heard hurt, pounding, there was a throbbing in the centre of his brain.

"I don't suppose it matters really," the girl started. "Yet I don't see a ring, you're not married?"

He frowned, where had that come from? "What? No...there was someone once but..."

"...it didn't work out?" Was that a smug look on her face?

"That's a polite way of saying it I guess. I work erratic hours. I have to follow my nose, sometimes at very short notice. I can be away from home for long periods of time. The life I lead isn't for everyone."

She looked out across the sea. "I know we've only just met and you find my comments somewhat forward, but I'm going to give you a once in a lifetime offer."

"Really?" He seemed genuinely perplexed.

"I am in Stateroom Eighteen. Do you think you can remember that? Shall we say half an hour?"

She ran a finger down his face. "Such soft, beautiful skin. And those cheeks of yours...to die for." She walked away, then stopped, turned, blew him a kiss.

Richardson watched her go; he stood alone for several moments before heading back inside the saloon. He bought himself a double whiskey. He was shaking and his heart was racing.

He didn't want to admit it but he needed a little Dutch courage.

***

He thought about knocking but what was the point? He was expected and she hadn't been backwards in coming forwards. He tried the handle: unlocked. He pushed the door open and stepped inside.

It was dark. The lights were out. The drapes were pulled tightly shut.

If his heart was racing back in the saloon, then it now threatened to beat right out of his chest; and as for that pain in his head, but he wasn't going to let that stop this happening, whatever *this* was.

Not that he minded, it was just unexpected.

He'd had to down several more whiskeys to give him that little extra Dutch courage.

"You came," a voice said in the darkness.

"Did you doubt that I would?" He paused. "It is a bit dark isn't it? Can we turn on a light?"

"I love the dark. I find it more...erotic; it adds a certain frisson."

Richardson took a deep breath. "I guess..."

Her laugh echoed around him...where exactly was she hiding?

"You have intrigued me James Richardson."

"Intrigued? I've never heard that before." He moved his head, was she moving around him? One minute she seemed to be on his right, the next then on his left. Why was she playing games? "Where are you?" he asked. He went to step forward but his head, he felt so dizzy, perhaps he had had too much of that bloody booze.

"I'm on the bed...waiting for you. Yearning for you."

She'd moved again.

Richardson took several breaths then cursed as he snagged his knee, there was a crashing sound – he'd knocked something over which had smashed on the floor.

"Be careful!" she warned. "You'll wake the neighbours and who knows how much that vase just cost me."

"I'll reimburse you..." He tried to laugh his stupidity off but that was more out of nervousness than anything else. He took off his coat, undid his waistcoat.

One more deep breath. There was a feint odour in the room; he hadn't really noticed it before but now with the doors and windows shut, it was becoming overpowering. It was in his nostrils, a tinge of something medicinal.

"You haven't even told me your name," he said as he slipped his braces over his shoulders, undid the buttons which fastened his trousers. He did his best to step out of them in the darkness without causing any more damage. He didn't have that much money on him...

"There is so much I haven't told you about myself but is that important? Especially right now, not at this moment. Now isn't the time..."

"Then what is this the time for?" His voice started to waiver. He had dreamed of something like this happening to him at least once in his life – the idea of being seduced by a beautiful woman, and boy was this girl beautiful – but now that he had the opportunity...

...he felt a hand on his shoulder, it was so sudden and unexpected that he almost dropped dead of shock.

"What's wrong?" she asked him. She was behind him now, her breath on his neck. His hair stood on end, goose bumps at war with his flesh.

"I'm fine," he replied yet his voice betrayed him, he was somewhat embarrassed.

She leant round, a hand on his chest. "You need to remain calm...breathe slowly...there is no harm meant."

He wanted to appear confident but knew he failed at that too.

"I want you to touch me."

He turned around, pulled down his underwear. He prayed he had this right and she wasn't playing with him.

He took a deep breath and reached out for her.

The girl moaned as his fingers skimmed her body, the top of her breast. He relaxed a little. She was naked too. This wasn't a game.

"You liked that?" he asked, doing it again, but this time (he hoped) a lot more expertly. Not just the top of her breast either. He tweaked her nipple.

She took his hand. "Let's take this to the bed," she whispered.

A gentle squeeze between his legs. He was excited, there was no doubting that.

The mattress squeaked as they climbed on. Her hands were on his waist, he mirrored her actions, they moved into each other. She held his neck, kissed it, then his cheeks, his lips.

That aroma again. Dry. Musty. He frowned, not though that she would see it. Their tongues were in each other mouths – probing, searching.

Her other hand was on his buttocks, she played with the soft hair between his legs.

"I love touching you," she said.

"I wish I could see you," he stated.

"Later, later, right now I want to make love to you."

His hand fell to her sex. She was wet. Soaking. She groaned as he probed the folds of her flesh.

"We need to do this now," he uttered, God he hoped he could last more than a few strokes.

She lay down, her legs opened wide; he kneeled between them then gently lowered himself onto her. His sinews and muscles stretched. She took him in hand, guided him deeper inside her, it hurt at first but then as the end of his penis hit the silky wetness he went with it, gliding the glans in and out. They breathed, they panted, together. She pulled him in closer, their bodies moved in unison.

"Fuck yeah," she groaned.

He was a little taken aback by the language but she wasn't wrong. He had never been as hard as this in his life and it only took several thrusts before the seed poured from him and into her.

"Damn it," he whispered, hoping she hadn't heard him.

The sweat was pouring and as he was still hard, rock hard, but she pushed him away, he fell face down onto the bed next to her.

"I wanted to go again," he stated, the disappointment obvious. His focus had been clear but now he had ejaculated, the migraine had come back with a vengeance.

She went to reply or at least he thought she did, but there was a loud knocking at the door, disturbing their post-love-making bliss.

"Who the hell is that?" he whispered.

"It's probably for you."

"Me?" the young man was perplexed. He turned over, stroked his penis, he was trying hard to stay...well...hard – in case she was up for it again. "No-one knows I'm here."

"Just do it will you?!" High tension in her voice.

"Alright, alright!" He climbed off the bed, scrambled around on the floor for something to cover his modesty. "I'm getting confused about all of this," he complained as he crossed the room, hitting his knee once more on the table.

The knocking became banging, Richardson searched around for the handle, unlocked the door. He pulled it open.

"Hello," a voice said.

It took a couple of moments for his eyes to adjust to the bright light. Richardson frowned.

Gustav. With two men by his side.

"What do you want?" Richardson asked just before a fist connected with his jaw, knocking him clean out.

He fell forward.

And as above, so below: everything went dark.

***

Someone slapped him across the face.

"Christ," he complained as he came round. He paused for a second then added. "Where am I?"

Swiftly he tried to take in where he was and what exactly was happening to him.

The room was bathed in an eerie electric blue light, like phosphorous, though the exact source of that he wasn't certain.

He was very frightened. Not though that he was going to let them see it, even if they knew it.

Who exactly were *they*?

Richardson tilted his head, to adjust his eyesight, he realised he probably had concussion, he felt woozy as if he wasn't entirely in his own body.

There were probably as many as twenty in the room with him. He tried to move but he was tied...no, strapped to something, a device of some kind!

A rack?

Possibly. He could just about work out that he was suspended from the ceiling, it didn't necessarily hurt but it was severely uncomfortable. Something dug in the back of his lower back, his thighs, and the back of his head.

He was naked too, but he tried not to pay that too much attention, there were other pressing things to be concerned over.

One thing in particular was the small metal table just in front of him, the top of which was covered in what appeared to be a black velvet cloth.

And on top of the cloth lay many surgical instruments.

Knives.

Scalpels.

Pliers.

Secateurs.

Needles, threads.

Even a saw!

There were glass tubes, Bunsen burners, hypodermic syringes and there another needle, burning bright in the centre of a blue flame.

Before him too was a box...no, a tea-chest. A crate! Covered by a large white sheet or tarpaulin. Perhaps six feet by six.

"What do you want?" His brain was finding it difficult to form sensible words.

"What do we want? What are we searching for?" a voice said. Far away. Distant.

The people, the acolytes or disciples whatever the fuck they were, turned.

Someone was coming, someone bathed from head to toe in white, like an angel.

"Doctor Papper," Richardson whispered, his heart sunk. He was wearing surgical scrubs.

"My my, you are observant." He was shed of his wheelchair; his legs worked perfectly fine. It had all been an act.

He was flanked by the girl (something different about her too, her hair brown and dirty – greasy; was it a wig?) – and Gustav, he was dressed similar to Papper.

Gustav went to the crate, lifted the sheet slightly, took a peek inside (how could he see anything of value in the dim light?).

"We need to hurry," he stated.

"Indeed we must. "Doctor Papper moved to the table, picked up a pair of gossamer gloves, and stretched them over his fingers. "Time conspires against us."

The girl, nonplussed, put a cigarette to her lips. What had happened to her? She looked so different now. Corrupt, he thought. He could he have screwed that? Her flesh, so much revealed now, pudgy, lumpy, covered in stretch lines...Jesus...it must have been the alcohol...

Papper tutted. "I really wish you wouldn't, you of all people should know better."

She returned a sarcastic smile but that didn't stop her lighting the cigarette and drawing in deeply, she moved to the wall, where there was a chair, she sat down.

"You asked me what I wanted," Doctor Papper started. "Simply put my boy, it is not what I want that is important, it is what you have."

"I'm...confused..." Richardson replied.

"I don't doubt that," Papper nodded. "You have a serum flowing around your body, heading towards your brain with every beat of your heart. A cocaine based concoction as it happens. I will inject some more direct into your bloodstream presently. I wasn't entirely sure of the right dosage initially – you are young, fit and healthy but you also have a problem with whiskey and after all you are *English* – that brings with it its own...uniqueness."

There was some laughter amongst the onlookers.

"My young friend, you might appreciate this but you have already played your role in tonight's proceedings...part of it anyway."

"How...?" Richardson's eyes were heavy, his limbs aching. He wanted to lie down and sleep, he was exhausted. But he couldn't. The strapping around his neck, wrists and ankles were digging deep into his skin, the flesh raw. Excruciating pain in his toes.

Something in his mouth, using his tongue he tried his best to fish it out, he coughed and spat to the floor. It was a piece of a tooth.

"I suspect I have you to thank for that," he said to Gustav who was paying him the minimal of attention, he was concentrating on whatever was going on in that large crate.

Richardson's eyes rolled into the back of his head. Damn, he was losing sense of both reality and his own perspective. Because of the cocaine? He was starting to see strange things – things he was dead sure weren't there but existing just beyond the realms of his imagination…

Gustav signalled to Doctor Papper that time was passing too quickly, Papper nodded solemnly.

"I'll explain this as simple as I can – I sought you out Mister Richardson. There was something about you, something that piqued my interest. Physically you are young, strong, athletic, attractive some would say. Your brain is enquiring too, intelligent. You have a way with words. Charisma. Well mannered. Indeed – a perfect specimen to father my grandson."

"I don't..."

Doctor Papper, using a small pair of tongs, reached into the flame, pulled out the needle. More than hot enough now for his purposes. With his other hand he lifted a glass syringe.

"I needed you to procreate with my daughter. Ever since her...accident...we weren't entirely positive whether she could physically bear children and there have been...challenges...but now your seed is inside her, hurtling towards fertilization."

"You're sick...do you know that...sick."

Papper smiled as he connected the needle to the syringe; picked up a small bottle full to the brim with a white milky liquid. He removed the stopper, stuck the needle inside, and pulled back the plunger. Liquid filled the syringe. Satisfied, he removed the needle from the bottle and approached.

"What are you going to do with that?" Richardson panicked.

The doctor grinned from ear to ear. "The same thing which you did to my daughter." He looked down between Richardson's legs. "Such a little prick."

"What the fu..."

The pain was intense, searing, right there in the centre of his forehead Doctor Papper jammed the hot needle. It hurt when it broke his skin; then as it went into the flesh, the thin muscle, teased the bone of his skull itself. The fluid injected in.

Richardson screamed as the needle was yanked from his head, a thin spray of blood covered Doctor Papper who wiped it away with his hand, licked his fingers as if it was inconsequential. He walked back to his table, dropped the syringe, the glass broke.

"What have you done…" the Englishman started – every nerve ending, every sensory receptor on fire. All about him he saw exploding colours, like bubbles, wind-chimes too played in his ears.

"That was easy," the girl stated as Richardson's head fell forward. He did try to right himself but his whole body was numb, like jelly. It was proving impossible to keep control of his faculties.

His brain was spinning, light, felt like his very essence was trying to fight free of his body. Sweat was pouring from his skin, bathing him in a sheen-like aura. Between his legs something was happening with his genitals, his scrotum tightened, he was erect. His soul wanted to separate itself from what made him *him.*

"Can't you hear that?" he asked but nobody was paying him the slightest attention.

Everyone had crowded around the crate, each holding a piece of the sheet that covered it.

He turned to the girl; she had lit another cigarette and was trying her hardest to blow smoke rings into the air – not that successfully either.

What was that?

Richardson keened his ears.

A drumbeat?

It was soft, far away at the start but then it was there. It was all around him, in him. It was him!

BOOM.
BOOM.
BOOM.
BOOM.

"You hear the witch drums don't you?" she sung. "It won't be long now..."

A bead of sweat dripped down Richardson's face onto his cheek. His muscles tensed.

"I am Lazarus..." he dribbled, saliva pouring from his mouth and other fluids (urine or semen, he wasn't entirely sure) from his penis.

Papper looked up. "No no no, my young friend, here is the one we will raise from the dead. You can rest easy; it is your death that will be his life..."

Richardson groaned. Everything was alive, he could see each and every molecule, every atom in the objects around him. Everyone – including himself – was immersed by a bright yellow light: a halo. Their insides had become illuminated; he felt electric. He was a god.

His jaw slackened; his lips numb. He tried to stretch his limbs, but that was impossible. He prayed that he kept control of his bowels but somehow he didn't believe that really mattered anymore.

The drumming in his head metamorphosed into a deep timbred chanting – it took some time to appreciate that the sound was no longer inside him but that it actually came from the crowd, those *acolytes*. They were swaying, dancing - perhaps he wasn't the only one hurtling towards a chemical nirvana; not the only one drifting in and out of consciousness...

***

...the covering had been removed from the crate. A spotlight shone down from the ceiling, lighting that and that only. The insides appeared to be fashioned from a cushioned velvet lining.

"What the fu..." Richardson uttered as his eyelids (when had they become so heavy?) fell.

Gustav and a second man leant inside, grabbed hold of something and very very carefully the sides of the crate were removed.

Something...no, someone was sitting there.

"Jesus...Jesus fucking Christ!" Richardson exclaimed.

Papper clicked his fingers. "Prepare another solution." One of the acolytes rushed to the table, did as he had been instructed.

Richardson thought he saw a man – well, at least it appeared to be male in form – but there were pieces...missing...there was a horrible stench too, like burnt skin; limbs appeared fused together. It looked like a man, but whilst it was naked – there was only a fleshy mass hanging between its legs.

"Isn't he beautiful?" Papper caressed the thing's scalp. "This is Emile. This is my son."

Richardson mumbled something but it was nonsensical.

"As you can see, he requires your assistance."

"Ass...st...ance?"

"Emile is...no longer himself...he has need of your skin, your flesh..."

The Englishman screamed as he felt something bite into his arm. He had been injected again; that warm sensation flowed around his body – his brain aflame.

"We have to have him whole again," Papper started. "And as that Irish whore helped Solange...you will aid Emile."

Richardson stared towards the ceiling. Thousands of insects crawled from the woodwork, transformed into birds, into monkeys, into ash that rained down upon him. He screeched in laughter.

Gustav helped Emile to his feet.

He turned towards his father who motioned with his head. Papper handed his son a scalpel; he held it in the stump of a hand. Emile limped forward.

That fucking stench – rancid piss shit and vomit was just the start – it was more than the scorched flesh: it was evil, pure unadulterated evil. Perfumed somewhat by a mixture of medical disinfectant and strong vanilla-based cologne.

Richardson stared into that one black eye (the other was a mangled mess)...was that pity he saw? Doubtful...

Emile's tongue darted out, flitted across the parched lower lip.

Some semblance of sound was gargled but Richardson had no idea what it meant.

"My son thanks you for the sacrifice you are about to make, for the pain you will endure."

Papper clicked his fingers, Gustav put on his gloves.

"Sacrrriiff...." More dribble, more spittle fell from Richardson's mouth.

Two disciples wheeled in a gurney, helped Emile onto it.

"Do I have to watch this?" Solange asked.

"Don't you want to see your brother resurrected?" Papper questioned.

"I'd rather not...I've been there before haven't I? I know what comes next. Resurrection is one thing but...actually witnessing it...I'll pass on that if it's all the same."

She stubbed out her cigarette, stood up; straightened her dress. She walked over to Richardson, kissed him on the forehead then on the lips.

"I thank you James Richardson for what you have given me and my brother." She tilted her head. "That's his name Emile: James Richardson. You must never forget that...we must never forget him."

Emile's stump of a left arm was extended, she gave it a gentle squeeze, headed towards the door.

Papper rubbed his hands together then picked up the large secateurs.

"They say that the first cut is the deepest don't they?"

Gustav prepared a swab. "We shall commence with his right lower leg."

Doctor Papper nodded. "That seems as best a place as any."

He opened and closed the secateurs, tested them for their strength. "Shall we begin?" He pulled up his mask, covering his mouth.

There was nothing for it, Richardson screamed as loudly as possible and then some.

Outside, a band began to play.

***

The blood was everywhere. The walls, the floor, the ceiling.

"Has it been a success?" one of the acolytes asked.

Papper wiped his brow, dropped the scalpel onto the table, it landed amongst the other metallic objects, they too stained with the red stuff.

He took off a glove. "Was it ever really in doubt?" He was exhausted.

Everyone stared at the two bodies.

Both bloody, one stripped of skin, of flesh and bone. The other – chest rising and falling. Eyes closed, bandages wrapped tightly, stitches hidden to keep the skin on top of flesh on top of bone.

"Emile?" Papper called. "Can you hear me?"

They waited with baited breath; prayed that what had transpired had been a success. Doctor Papper was hoping to prove that what had occurred with Solange was not just a one off - and if conditions were right, then it could be done time and time again.

Many of them didn't quite understand the science behind all of it, perhaps it was just mumbo-jumbo when he had spoken to them in that Paris sanctuary about raising the dead, evoking demons and conversing with Lucifer himself.

They had seen what he had done for his daughter...but this was different, this was almost wholesale transferring of one body onto another.

Not just the grafting of skin!

The possibilities were limitless. The money they had paid to him, to fund his works was more than worth it...they stood to make a million times what they put in.

That Richardson had perished, that was never in doubt. No-one could be sure exactly when his heart gave way and his soul departed, but depart it had and by then several of his limbs had been dislocated, broken, hacked away and transplanted onto Emile's tender frame.

Muscles, flesh and skin also.

Papper had been correct, he had been the perfect choice.

Even the genitals – Papper had expressed grave concerns about their size and weight and didn't want to leave his son with a disadvantage but Gustav (rightly so!) pointed out that beggars couldn't be choosers and besides which, they were damn sight better than what the boy currently had hanging between his legs.

The tension in the room was palpable.

Papper frowned, it had to work – it just had to work. This was his life...his reputation at stake.

"Emile, if you can hear me, open your eyes. It is your father. I am holding my hand out for you my son, reach for me, return to me. Return to me my darling Emile. Step into the light, unwrap that cloak of darkness which has embraced you for far too long."

Nothing happened for several moments.

But then: "Look," someone shouted. "His eyes! He's opening his eyes!"

This exclamation was correct. Slowly, ever so slowly and only slightly, the boy's eyes opened.

"Don't crowd him, give him room to breathe!" Gustav cried.

Papper took a step forward. "My beautiful boy, can you hear me?"

Emile, using Richardson's eyes, looked about him. A strange look on his face, his mouth opened; the lips attempting to form words.

"What was that son? What was that you said?" Papper leant down.

"Father," Emile asked. "What have you done?"

Papper appeared bemused. "I don't understand, what do you mean?"

"You should have let me die...you shouldn't have let me live. You should never have brought me back...there is a shadow here father, I can see it...it hovers close..."

The door flew open, Solange stood there. Everyone turned to her. The brass number '16' on the wood glinted in the bright light suddenly shining in from outside.

She looked terrified. There were noises, a commotion, shouting, yelling from behind her. She was soaking wet.

"Father, we must..."

However, that was all she managed to say before she was suddenly catapulted into the room.

That was when the real screaming started…

***

It had been a tiring couple of weeks. Doctor Oldham wiped his face, replaced his glasses; stared into the flames. He supposed he needed to check in on that English reporter. It had been touch and go for a while; he'd never seen a body that had suffered so much trauma, though it now seemed that he had turned the corner. A very long road to recovery awaited him but at least the first steps had been taken.

He left his office, meandered along the corridor. He'd visit the reporter then it was time to call it a night. He needed some rest. He needed to get home to his wife and family – he'd been neglecting them recently, of course they understood but it was time to get back to some kind of normality.

He pushed the double door open, then stopped.

"What's going on here?" Several nurses were changing the bed sheets.

"Sorry doctor, can I help?" Matron asked.

"Yes, where is my patient – Richardson?"

She looked confused, went to the end of the bed, picked up the clipboard, flipped through the pages. "He's been transferred to a private sanatorium, out of the city."

Oldham shook his head. "No, no, no. This isn't right. Who ordered the transfer? He's not a well man. He shouldn't have been moved."

The matron pulled him out of earshot of her nurses. "You did."

He snatched the clipboard from her. "I did nothing of the sort..." He looked down at the manifest, there was his name signed as giving permission for Richardson's discharge and transfer. It looked like his signature anyway.

"Is something wrong?" she asked stoically.

He stared at her for several moments before offering her a thin smile. "No, you're right. I did sign this off...my apologies...I'm very tired." He handed her back the clipboard, turned on his heels and exited.

It was all becoming so confusing recently, first all that business with that nurse...where had she vanished too? They'd discovered her dirty uniform stashed away in one of the service cupboards. He knew it was hers right away. The stench of smoke was so overpowering...

...he needed a vacation, he'd speak to the registrar in the morning.

He went back into his office, opened up his drawer, took out his keys, his wallet; removed his lab-coat, picked up his jacket and was about to leave when he noticed there was a folded piece of white card lying there on his jotter.

There was a strange gold symbol and a number '16' on one side and on the other, an elegant flowing signature.

"Doctor Ernst Papper," he said aloud. Just who in hell was Doctor Papper...?

MAIDEN VOYAGE

by Sylvia Shults

Karl Sander hated Tuesdays.

He sighed, a long gusty exhalation, and fought the urge to ruffle-comb his fingers through his hair. High-ranking Reich officials were supposed to look neat and presentable at all times, even if they were only scientists. The Einstein look was long out of fashion.

He frowned down at the mortality reports. They always arrived in a tidy stack, placed precisely in the middle of his 'in' box every Tuesday at 8 am by his over-efficient secretary. He usually started leafing through the stack around two in the afternoon. By about 4:30, they were scattered across his desk in a whirlwind of ink and paper.

The figures were all stored in the massive electronic guts of the Health System, but the Director of the Ministry for Public Health had decided that it would be helpful to have the figures printed out, for Karl to go over every week.

Helpful it may have been, fun it most certainly was not.

Karl appreciated that his job in the Health System required him to do his part in studying mortality rates around the world - he had the United States, Dietrich Hauser, in the office across the hall, had Europe (as bad as his part of the job was, Karl was glad he didn't have Hauser's assignment. He had relatives all over Europe).

Karl even appreciated his secretary printing out the reports for him every week. Without the stack of papers in front of him, he'd probably ignore the reports for weeks on end – not the kind of work ethic that had propelled him to his lofty position in the Ministry.

And he was Teutonic to the bone. The meticulous nature of the work was a pleasure. It was the task itself that bothered him. Every Tuesday, for at least two hours, he had to wade through an entire country's laundry list of death: Drownings, suicides, accidents, disease, gunfire, house fires, and stabbings – it was all here, every week.

Murder took up a lot of the reports, as did Karl's personal horror: cancer.

In short, all the myriad ways in which a nation's citizens could be killed, or die all on their own, were printed out and placed on Karl Sander's desk every week.

And every week, Karl had to go through and read it, cover to plastic cover.

He *hated* Tuesdays.

But at least this Tuesday was almost over.

Karl gathered up the scattered pages of the mortality report, straightened them, marked them 'read', and tossed the pile into his 'out' box.

Done for another week, thank god.

On the way home, Karl had time to think. He rested his head against the soft leather of the seat, and listened to the quiet, satisfying hum of the Benz's motor as he drove home.

Another Tuesday report out of the way.

He couldn't wait to get home to Rosalinde and Lukas. Reading the mortality reports did that to him, made him want to rush right home, gather his wife and son into his arms, and hold them tightly, the ancient magic of the family circle protecting them all from harm.

It wasn't so much the deaths that bothered him – he had spent most of his career becoming an expert on infectious diseases – as it was the dry, dispassionate reporting of the facts.

He almost resented the Americans for dying in such numbers and making his life hellish for two hours every Tuesday afternoon. He realized that America was a client nation of Germany, and that Germany had a responsibility, as she did to the rest of the world, to protect America, to look after the weaker nation's interests. It had always seemed to Karl, though, that a nation that big should certainly be able to take care of itself.

It wasn't that he disliked Americans as a group, or as individuals. It was just the way of the world in this modern age. The world had a certain comforting order to it these days. Germany was the undisputed world leader, an empress among nations, and America was the supplicant, depending on the good graces of her powerful patron.

And Germany had been gracious. The terms of the Allied surrender in the Great War had been stern, but fair. Under Germany's patronage, all of Europe had prospered, even the little island country of Britain. America had been allowed to share in that prosperity.

But lately, Karl had begun to question his country's kindly attitude. Why should Germany have to shoulder the responsibility for the rest of the planet's wellbeing?

The United States had never been a nation of power, but then again, it had never gotten the chance.

Karl daydreamed every once in a while about a different world, a world in which America stood on its own, needing no help from Germany or any other nation. A world in which he didn't have to look at those damn mortality reports every week.

He turned down the lovely, tree-lined street, and immediately felt better. His home, a large house set well back from the quiet street in an impeccably maintained yard, was more than just a dwelling to him.

It was a gracious retreat, a place of refuge from the often stressful world he found himself living in from day to day. He pulled into the long driveway, pressed the button to raise the automatic garage door, and guided the purring car into his spot in the garage. He shut off the engine, clicked the door remote again, and headed into the house as the garage door rattled smoothly closed, shutting out the world for another night.

Karl stepped into the kitchen and smiled. This was always the best part of his day. He closed his eyes, trying to guess what Rosalinde had fixed for supper by the delicious smells that hung enticingly in the air.

"Braised spareribs, buttered noodles, fresh peas, and homemade bread. And for dessert, peach cobbler."

"Aah, so *that's* what I'm smelling," Karl opened his eyes. Rosalinde was standing in front of him, cool and elegant as always.

"Probably. It's still in the oven."

She was amazing, this wife of his. With grocery service available at the touch of a computer screen, Rosalinde preferred to go to the markets herself, picking out the freshest ingredients and transforming them into meals fit for Kaiser Hermann. She even did her own baking – not that this was much of a chore with the bread machine, but oh, the results were heavenly.

Rosalinde moved past him to the counter. She unwrapped the loaf of bread, took a knife from the rack, and began cutting thick slices. Karl slipped his arms around her from behind, nuzzling the back of her neck at the base of her upswept hair. Wisps of her hair tickled his nose, and he inhaled deeply, breathing in her scent mingled with the homey smell of the fresh-baked bread.

"Let go," Rosalinde said, but Karl heard the smile in her voice.

"Why should I?"

"I have to get a plate for the bread."

"Well, in that case ..."

He nipped gently at the back of her neck, and planted a kiss there before letting her go.

"Careful. You don't want to let Lukas catch you doing that," Rosalinde teased.

"Why not? He's used to this mushy stuff. He knows his parents love each other."

"Mmm – yes they do," she replied, kissing him. "Go call him for supper, would you? He's doing his homework in the living room."

Karl wandered down the hallway to the living room. He found Lukas sprawled on the couch in front of the viewing screen.

The boy had slouched his lean body in the typical, relaxed pose of adolescence, with his arms crossed behind his head and his long legs propped up on the low table in front of the couch.

Karl felt a swell of love and pride. Lukas was a great kid; handsome, good in school, with a bright future ahead of him.

He and Rosalinde had done a decent job raising the boy, Karl thought.

Of course, Lukas did have a spark of the rebel in him. At his last haircut, he had insisted on getting the latest popular sports symbol – a tilted cross with extra arms jutting out at each end – shaved into his short hair.

Karl didn't follow sports, so he didn't see the appeal of the symbol. But that wasn't so bad. He supposed he could forgive his teenage son the idiosyncrasies of youth.

"Television? This is what they give for homework in high school these days?"

Lukas looked up briefly. "Hi, Pop. It's not a show or anything. We have to watch the news every night for a week. I picked a good night," he said with a grin. "They're talking about the Mars launch. You gotta watch some of this, it's really ace."

Lukas slid over to make room on the couch, and Karl sat down next to him.

"Thank you, Trina. I'm here at Germany's moon base with the men and women of the High Ground crew."

The reception was clear; since the establishment of the moon base in 1999, communications had been improving, so now a news broadcast from the base was as crisp and static-free as a report from the local soccer stadium.

"Following the space program's motto, 'Take the high ground', these brave men and women are preparing for the world's first manned flight to Mars. If all goes according to schedule, we should be seeing shuttle flights to the Red Planet in three years, isn't that right, Commander?"

"Yes, the plan calls for a regular shuttle service to Mars by 2040. We're very excited to be a part of the High Ground program. I'd just like to thank the Kaiser for his confidence in my crew."

There was more: the reporter looking around with ill-concealed awe at the clean, shining lines of the space station, the commander of the flight firmly giving his congratulations to his crew and to the support staff that had made it all possible.

Lukas sat as if glued to the couch, hypnotized by the thought of travelling beyond the stars. Karl knew how the boy felt. He felt a little patriotic thrill go through him every time he heard a reference to Germany's space program. It was something to be proud of, to have made it to the moon, and now to be looking beyond, to be the first humans to set foot on another planet.

"Guys, supper! Remember?" Rosalinde's voice called them both back to earth. Karl gave his son a sheepish grin.

"By the way, supper's ready."

***

Karl spent the evening in his study.

Next to the bedroom he and Rosalinde shared, it was his favorite room in the house. Bookshelves lined the dark-panelled walls, mute testimony to one of Karl's passions.

A bar, with polished glasses neatly stacked, stood discreetly in the corner. Karl stood contemplating one of the pictures that hung on the wall.

It was a painting, a quiet evening scene, with lit streetlamps casting a gentle glow on the pedestrians hurrying home at the end of the day. It wasn't a very good painting, but Karl found that he could relate to the feeling of easy peace that glowed from the scene. Besides, family legend held that the artist had been a distant ancestor of his, a long-lost uncle or cousin by the name of Hitler.

A knock on the door of the study brought him out of his daydream. A short, well-built man opened the door and peered in. "I'm not interrupting anything, am I?"

"Nikolas! No, you never do, you ought to know that by now. Come on in." Karl went to the bar. "Can I get you anything? Spiced brandy?"

"As always." Nikolas smiled.

"Nothing but the best, of course." Karl poured two glasses and handed one to his friend.

Nikolas took a sip and nodded his approval. He wandered over to one of the large chairs that stood next to the fireplace and sat down.

"I saw Lukas in the kitchen. He was having a piece of Rosalinde's peach cobbler. He offered me some, but I'm still full from Margot's fine dinner." As if on cue, there was another knock on the door.

"Pop? You busy?"

Karl raised an eyebrow at Nikolas, who shrugged. "No, Lukas, come on in."

Lukas wandered into the study carrying a glass of milk and sat down across from Nikolas. Karl leaned comfortably up against the mantelpiece, hiding a smile. He knew how much Lukas wanted to be included in the grown-ups' world. "So what's up, son?"

"Not much. I'm taking a break from a paper I'm writing for school."

"What's the paper about?" Nikolas asked.

"It's for my Twentieth Century History class. We're supposed to do a paper outlining how Imperial Germany rose to power."

Nikolas took a sip of brandy. "And what's your opinion?"

Lukas leaned forward eagerly. "I think it was because of those two deadly plagues that hit the United States during the early twentieth century." He looked up at Karl. "Help me out here if I'm wrong, Pop. There was that huge anthrax plague in 1912. A million people died in that one. It wiped out the entire eastern seaboard, which was where most of the industrial power was located. Then, just six years later, the influenza pandemic struck, killing half a million people just in America alone. That's a million and a half dead in less than ten years. The United States never really recovered from that." He paused, as if to shudder with the delicious horror of a tragedy over a century old.

Karl shifted his weight, suddenly uncomfortable with this discussion of mass death. "Yes, but Germany lost plenty of soldiers to influenza during the Great War. Why were we able to win, while the Allies lost?"

Lukas hesitated and bit at his lower lip, thinking.

"Go on, Luke," Nikolas encouraged him. "You're on the right track. Don't let your father throw you off. It's your paper, after all."

Lukas nodded; then looked back to Karl. "Since the epidemics had done so much damage to the United States, they weren't able to fight in the Great War at all. Then, in 1934 when Germany started the Blitzkrieg and took over Poland and France, America was still too weak to help when Britain tried to stop us."

"Well, it was a little more complicated than that, but you've got the right idea. Don't forget your references. I've got plenty of books in here you can use for your bibliography."

"Thanks. I'll come in tomorrow and get some. The paper's not due for another week." Lukas drained his glass and stood. "Guess I better get back to the grind."

"That's the spirit." Karl watched him go, a faint, fond smile on his face. As the door closed behind Lukas, he turned to his friend. "He resembles his great-grandmother, you know.

"You've mentioned it before," Nikolas said. "She must have been a remarkable woman."

"She was," Karl agreed. "Grandma did a little of everything. She was very talented. She was a writer, an artist, a musician...she sang beautifully. She actually went to school for music, did I ever tell you that? She kept it up, even while she was raising her family. Who knows how far she could have gone if she hadn't developed cancer?" Karl took a swig of his brandy. Instead of warming him gently as it usually did, it traced a line of fire down his throat.

"That's the trouble with Germany today, Nikolas," Karl continued in a low, pained voice. "We were methodical and efficient enough to build an empire in a century and a half, and to put a base on the moon. Our technological superiority made us into a world power. We can create empires, and build nuclear power plants to run them, but we can't prevent people who work there from getting cancer from the radiation. We can't prevent it, and we can't defeat it."

Nikolas spoke softly. "You were close to her, weren't you?"

"Yes. Yes, I was close to her." Karl's voice was rough with remembered pain. "I had to watch her waste away and die, and there was nothing I could do for her. Nothing." He took another swallow of brandy.

Both men were silent for a while, the soothing silence of long-time friends who sometimes have no need for words. Then Karl spoke.

"How's your department doing?"

Nikolas shifted his weight, and the chair squeaked comfortably underneath him.

"Fine, fine. We're doing several Zeitsehen jumps a month now. Only official business runs, of course - I dread the day when some Hohenzollern relative comes to me with a request for a sightseeing trip to the Roman Empire for his daughter's sixteenth birthday." He chuckled.

Karl sat down. He picked up a pen from the table next to him and started to run it through his fingers, turning it end over end in mindless repetition. His tone was deliberately casual as he spoke.

"I'll be contacting your office soon. I've been looking to start a series of survey trips to study major plagues. Now that we've got the entire vaccination schedule done, I might just start with that anthrax-influenza double whammy in the United States."

Nikolas set his glass down and fixed Karl with a stern glare. "What are you planning?"

Karl's eyes widened. "Planning? I'm not planning anything. I've been thinking about the survey, that's all, the Minister has been after me lately to get started on it, and I just thought..."

Nikolas cut him off. "Come on, Karl, don't give me that. You and I have been friends since we were Luke's age. Now tell me what's going on."

Karl took a deep breath. He put the pen down and leaned forward. "Right. According to Lukas, the first blow to the power of the United States was the anthrax plague. How did that start?"

"Well, as far as anyone can tell, it was brought over from Europe on the Titanic."

"Okay. But what if the Titanic had never made it to New York? What if it had – oh, I don't know – hit an iceberg or something and sank before it ever got there?"

Nikolas stared at him. "Karl, the Zeitsehen machines were never meant to be used to change history."

Karl ignored the implied warning in his friend's tone. "The Titanic's regular run was across the North Atlantic. It's entirely possible she could have hit an iceberg on one of her trips."

"Karl, it *did* hit a berg. October, 1930-something, remember? It hit a berg head-on, part of the ship filled with water, and it barely limped into port. Then five years later, it was grazed by a torpedo in the Adriatic. My dad's grandfather was on the Titanic when it was a hospital ship in the final days of the Blitzkrieg. The damn thing was unsinkable!"

"All I'm saying is that it's possible, if she hit a big iceberg, or hit it just right..."

"What about the *history*, Karl?" Nikolas interrupted in a fierce whisper. "You're willing to take the chance of changing a hundred and thirty years of time? Why?"

Karl's gaze was steady ad he stared into his friend's eyes. "For Lukas. I'm doing it for Lukas, and for my grandmother. He never knew her, Nikolas. What if I *could* change history, let the United States catch up to us just a bit? Let *them* build nuclear power plants. Let *their* people die of cancer." His voice was firm, but his fingernails were carving painful crescents into his palms.

Nikolas met Karl's stare. "I can't believe you're actually asking me to help you change over a century of events that have already happened. There are laws against the misuse of the machines, you know. We could both get in serious trouble."

"I'm not asking you to help. All I'm asking you to do is push a button. You do it every day; it's your job, isn't it? What's the difference?"

"There are *laws,*" Nikolas repeated stubbornly.

Karl stood up and started pacing, unable to meet his friend's eyes any longer. "Then let me sweeten it for you. I know how much you love being a Zeitsehen technician. How would you like to move up to the head of the class? As one of the higher officials at Public Health, I can make recommendations as to who should be promoted in any department. I can get you promoted to Senior Tech status. You wouldn't just be pushing the buttons any more. You'd be in charge of scheduling trips yourself. You could even deny people travel rights if you wanted to. Then that Hohenzollern heiress would have to kiss her Roman orgy trip from Daddy goodbye, wouldn't she?"

Karl could feel Nikolas's gaze on him as he paced. "You're serious about this, aren't you?"

He stopped and faced his friend. "I want Lukas to meet his great-grandmother."

"You say you're already planning a trip to the United States in 1912 to study the outbreak of the anthrax-influenza pandemic?"

Karl's eyes were bright. "Yes. All I want you to do is send me to England instead of America. How hard can it be?"

Nikolas shook his head. "I don't know what you're exactly up to Karl." He held up a hand. "I don't *want* to know. Just tell me one thing, tell me you'll be careful."

Karl silently held out his hand. Nikolas stood, holding his friend's gaze with his own. After a long moment, he took Karl's hand and shook it in a firm grip. He left without another word.

***

Over the next few weeks, Karl immersed himself in the culture of 1912. His trip back to study the plague caused little comment in the department. In fact, Karl's director was pleased that Karl had finally started his project.

The time machine that the Germans had perfected worked well. It would get you where (and when) you wanted to go; the trip was a matter of moments.

Everyone who used it, though, was responsible for their own research into their chosen time period. Karl decided on the persona of an upper-class German gentleman, not a far stretch from real life.

He borrowed several outfits and a travelling trunk from the Zeitsehen library. He left the trunk and most of the suits in his office, but one night, he took one of the outfits home with him.

He tried it on and stood in front of the full-length mirror in the bedroom, admiring the figure he cut, trying to get into the mindset of the period.

"That'll do," he muttered, trying to imagine himself as an arrogant, worldly Edwardian gentleman. He lifted his chin, picturing a ship's steward hurrying to grab his bags to take them on board the mighty liner. He was actually looking forward to that. The luggage he had picked out, a good solid steamer trunk, felt like it weighed half a ton.

Karl checked out a few books from the Zeitsehen library as well, to brush up on his English. He'd taken two years of it in college, to get his language requirement out of the way, but he was rusty. He hoped his strong German accent would cover his ignorance of syntax.

In addition to his language research, Karl read everything he could find on the Titanic. There wasn't much. Most of it dealt with Titanic's brush with disaster in 1934. There was a little information, not much, on her service as a hospital ship. Apparently, being grazed by a torpedo was only worth one paragraph in the history books. He'd have thought that a ship that had proven her unsinkability - twice - deserved a little more respect.

He hadn't neglected the practical side of his preparation, either. He arranged for a full series of vaccinations just to be safe.

His one concession to modern research was to bring along a BacFinder. The hand-held device was not only a computer on which he could record his findings, but also a powerful microbe detector.

It was calibrated for both anthrax and influenza. In the presence of the deadly germs, the small display screen would glow a muted blue to alert the operator. The device was small, about the size of a well-stuffed billfold or a tin of breath mints, but Karl realized that it was at once his most valuable possession and his greatest liability. This was the anachronism that could get him into serious trouble in 1912. His use of the detector had to be short, infrequent, and above all, discreet.

On the night before he left, Karl lay in bed watching Rosalinde brush her hair. The only light in the room came from the small lamp on the bedside table. The soft glow of the lamp shone on her dark hair as she pulled the brush through her hair with sure strokes. Her hair lay like oil on the white satin of her robe. She put the brush down and reached up to begin braiding it, but Karl stopped her.

"No, leave it down tonight. For me."

Rosalinde smiled and got up from her chair. She came towards the bed, the robe swirling gently around her smooth calves. Karl turned the covers down and patted the bed.

"Care to join me?"

Rosalinde slanted a look at him from beneath lowered lids. "Can you stand it?"

"I'll try."

She untied the robe and let it slip from her shoulders. Underneath she was smooth, perfect, her body sculpted with exercise and healthy living.

She knelt on the bed, and Karl reached for her. He twined his fingers through her soft hair, bringing it to his face to inhale her scent. She made a contented noise deep in her throat.

Suddenly Karl wanted to call the department, to call the Director himself, wake him up if he had to. He didn't want to go tomorrow. All he wanted to do was stay here with his wife, to lose himself in her body, to make love to her all night long and into the next day, to stay safe with her and not travel into the unknown past. The past was dead, he didn't belong there. He didn't want to travel there, a stranger in a dead land.

Then the feeling of panic faded.

He felt himself growing hard, confident. He took Rosalinde in his arms and laid her gently down onto the bed. He stroked her dark hair back from her face, loving the way it framed her head in soft waves on the pillow. He eased inside her, hearing her gasp of pleasure, reveling in every caught breath, every gentle answering thrust of her hips, every heavy, drowsy blink of her eyes.

Then her breath came faster, her teeth catching at her bottom lip with desire. He felt her liquid heat grasping him, quickening underneath him until he was close to exploding. He held back, barely, until he felt her spasms of release and heard her shuddering cry of ecstasy. Only then did he allow himself his own arching, panting cries, sobbing her name into the fragrant waves of her hair.

When they were finished, he held her until she fell asleep. As he listened to her breathing grow slow and regular against his bare chest, Karl thought again about tomorrow's trip. He realized with a sense of growing wonder that he would be back in this bed tomorrow night, his arms around his wife, in exactly this same way. But before he returned, he would have made a journey of a hundred years and more. He closed his eyes. It hurt his head to think about it too much.

When he was sure Rosalinde was asleep, Karl got out of bed without disturbing her. He slipped a pair of boxer shorts on, and padded downstairs in his bare feet. In his study, working by the light of the full moon that shone in through the window, he opened the cabinet under the bar. He took out two bottles of spiced brandy and put them on top of the bar. Then he crossed the study to his desk and took out a piece of paper and a pen. He scribbled a note: *These are for Nikolas.* He left the note propped against the bottles, and went back upstairs to bed.

***

The next morning Karl woke up alone. Rosalinde was a morning person, and this was her time for herself. He lay in bed for a while, just thinking. He felt a shiver of excitement. He recognized the feeling.

It was the same delicious anticipation he felt before heading off on vacation, or on any long trip. Still, this time was different. The feeling now was more intense, somehow more important. Today, when he left on his journey, he'd be travelling through time.

The feeling persisted on his way in to work. Now that he had committed to the journey, he couldn't help but wonder if his trip would actually change things in this Germany he knew.

On his way into the building, Karl nodded to the uniformed security guard at the front desk. A little voice in his mind wondered, "When I get back, will the guard at the door still be black? Will he still speak his German with an English accent?"

He went to his office to collect his trunk, and lugged it over to the part of the building complex where Nikolas worked. He was sweating by the time he got there, and he sat for a while in the receptionist's area before getting out his papers. When he'd gotten his breath back, he went up to the receptionist's desk.

"I'm here for the Z-Seven. My name's Doctor Karl Sander; I have an appointment."

The pretty receptionist smiled and pointed. "It's just down that hallway. Show your travel pass to the guard at the door."

Karl nodded and set off down the hall. The unsmiling guard stopped him at the door.

"Papers please."

Karl unfolded the papers, which were creased and a little sweaty from their stay in his inside pocket. The guard peered at the Director's signature, gave a brief nod, and opened the door.

Karl stepped through the door and lugged his steamer trunk alongside. He found himself in a room the size of a warehouse. Sounds echoed dully off the metal trusses in the ceiling. An enormous machine squatted in the middle of the concrete floor. Karl immediately began to doubt his reasons for wanting to trust his life to that insectile monstrosity.

"There you are. I've been waiting for you!" Nikolas came hurrying up to him. He grabbed one end of the steamer trunk and helped Karl carry it around to the door of the time machine. He set his end down with a grunt. "You know, when you get to 1912, you'll be able to hire a porter."

"I intend to."

Karl looked up at the time machine. Seen up close, it lost none of its menace. Karl walked around the machine, stalling for time – the thought almost made him smile.

He knew it was ridiculous to be afraid. German scientists, the most efficient in the world, had tested and retested time travel theories. This machine, and other like it, had been in use for over thirty years.

Time, and history, would go on as they always had, no matter what he did in the past. He'd probably end up having this same conversation with Nikolas the next time he used the machine to travel.

The only difference was that next time, his grandmother might be alive. That hope was why he'd gotten up and come in to work this morning.

Karl noticed a plaque on the side of the machine. He stepped forward for a closer look.

Z-7

Zeitsehenmaschine – Version 7

Dedicated with gratitude to Father Alfredo Pellegrino Ernetti

"Nikolas?"

"Yes?" His friend was at a nearby control panel, presumably making last-minute adjustments to the machine.

"What does this plaque mean?"

"Oh, that? All Z-machines have one. Father Ernetti invented the first of the Z-series. He was an Italian monk who lived in the last century. I think he was born in 1926. Anyway, he was a Classics scholar, very interested in something called *prepolyphony*. That's a fancy word for ancient music, specifically the music composed between 1400 BC and 1000 AD. He was obsessed with finding out what the Roman play *Thyestes* sounded like when played on the musical instruments of the time."

"Sounds like a crackpot," Karl muttered.

"Yes, but his train of thought actually made sense. Ernetti had studied the writings of Pythagoras, who in about 350 BC theorized that the sounds of music, after they're played, break down in such a way that they become atom-like particles that are then stored in naturally occurring energy fields. Father Ernetti took Pythagoras's theory a couple of steps further. He figured that since time equals energy, and energy is neither created nor destroyed, all time must exist somewhere."

"So all the music that's ever been played must be floating around out there too."

"Exactly. He wanted to build a time machine to help him create audio-visual records of musical performances that would otherwise be lost in time. He persuaded twelve scientists to help him build his machine, which he called the Chronovisor. They worked on it from the 1950s to the 1990s. A prototype was developed in the early 1970s. In 1972, one of the scientists leaked a photograph to the press. It was a picture of Christ dying on the cross."

"I'll bet that got everyone's attention."

"Oh, the Church was furious. They said time travel was blasphemy; that mere mortals shouldn't be able to look back on the mysteries of the past. So Father Ernetti basically defected from the church. In the end, I guess his music was more important to him."

"Lucky for us."

"Right. Now just let me check something else." Nikolas punched a few more numbers into the computer keypad. "You're well within the limits. That's good."

His friend's impromptu history lesson had the ring of repetition to it, as though Nikolas had explained it a hundred times to a hundred nervous passengers. Karl didn't care. He was grateful for the distraction. "You mean there's a limit to how far back I can go?"

"Well, yes, in a sense. You can't go back less than a hundred years, about three generations. That assures that you can't change your own history on a purely personal level." Nikolas gave him a stern look.

"What, like killing my grandfather so I end up not being born?" Karl tried to lighten the moment.

"That, and things like assassinating the Reich Chancellor in infancy, all the things that science fiction writers love to play with. It makes great reading – that's what led me to a career as a Z-tech – but for practical purposes, it's just safer this way."

"Safer. Right." Karl eyed the Z-Seven warily. "You've, ah, tested this machine lately?"

Nikolas laughed. "Will you stop being so squeamish? This particular machine has been in service for six years. I transport people two or three times a month, and every four months, it gets a complete and thorough inspection. It's perfectly safe." He leaned closer. "Karl, I promise you it's as safe as that unsinkable ship you'll be getting on shortly."

Karl nodded, but stayed where he was. "Can you at least tell me how it works?"

"Not unless you've got several months to spare for an in-depth lecture on quantum physics. Are you really interested, or are you just playing for time?"

"A little of both," Karl admitted.

"Oh, come on, do you have to know how electricity works in order to flip on a light switch?"

"I think this is a little more complicated than turning on a light, and I'd like a bit of explanation, if you don't mind."

Nikolas sighed. "Fine. Get into the pod and I'll give you the short version while you're getting comfortable."

He turned to the machine and pressed a series of numbers on the pad next to the door. The door opened with a soft *shuush* of air. He helped Karl carry the trunk into the transportation chamber. There was enough room in the chamber for several people. With Karl, Nikolas, and the luggage, the space was cozy but comfortable.

"All right, the short version: quantum teleportation is, to put it simply, information transmitted at the speed of light without using wires or cables. Stand here. You'll need to put your feet right on those outlines on the floor. Teleportation depends on a property called entanglement. Physicists like to call it 'spooky action at a distance', and it is kind of spooky." He stood the trunk on end and wrestled it into position.

"Sometimes two particles that are a very long distance apart are connected somehow. We don't understand it, but we've learned how to use it. The properties of one particle affect the properties of the other. Entanglement means that if you tickle one, the other one laughs."

Nikolas turned to Karl, eyes bright with anticipation. "It also means that once I leave this chamber, go out into the lab, and press a few buttons, you'll end up in our lab in London, in 1912."

"That's the short version, huh?" Karl tried to smile, but his face felt tight.

"Just relax," Nikolas said. "Once you've finished your research, go to the Washington Zeitsehen lab. It's not that far from New York, where the Titanic will dock. It's actually less than a week's travel in a car of that time. Tell the tech you want to come back to this date. I'll be waiting right here for you, and tonight, we'll sit in your study and toast the success of your first time-trip." Nikolas put out his hand, and Karl shook it.

"Remember to relax," Nikolas repeated as he went out the door. "Just hold still. When the buzzer sounds, you'll be there. You might want to close your eyes for a moment or so. I'm told it helps."

Karl nodded and closed his eyes. He heard Nikolas whisper, "Good luck." Then the door closed with the finality of a coffin lid, and Karl was alone.

He took a deep breath and let it out slowly, hoping he wasn't disobeying Nikolas's order to hold still. Brilliant flashes of light strobed across his closed eyelids, and he felt a queasy lurch in the pit of his stomach. Then the buzzer blared. He had arrived.

Karl opened his eyes. He seemed to be in one piece. He reached out and pressed the large exit button next to the door. The door whooshed open. Lugging his trunk behind him, he stepped out into the laboratory, and into 1912.

He blinked in astonishment. He found himself in an exact duplicate of the room he'd just left. Even the plaque on the machine thanking Father Ernetti for his contribution to science was identical. The technician, however, was not Nikolas. He was younger, in his late twenties, with jet black hair cut in a style Karl recognized as old-fashioned, and a friendly smile.

"Welcome to 1912!" He looked down at his computer monitor. "You must be Doctor Karl Sander."

Karl nodded, and the technician continued. "I'm Simon Weisenthal. I'm the tech on this end, and the resident historian. Could you open your trunk, please?"

Karl undid the latches and heaved open the lid. Weisenthal went through the contents in a quick but thorough inspection. "Looks good. You must really know your history, Doctor Sander."

"I did a lot of research before I came. That helped."

"We historians on this end appreciate it, believe me. Historical accuracy has been crucial to hiding our presence through the ages. Now I do realize you're on a research trip. Do you have any anachronisms you wish to declare?"

Karl showed him the BacFinder, and explained how it worked. Weisenthal frowned at it, but handed it back to him. "You've got the proper paperwork for it. Just be careful. Now, may I see your wallet, please?"

Karl raised an eyebrow, but reached into his pants pocket and took out his wallet. He handed it to Weisenthal, who took it and emptied the contents out onto a table. "Let's see what we've got here. Anastasia!"

A young woman came into the lab, and Weisenthal handed her Karl's ID papers. "Make up some business cards for Doctor Sander. Do twenty of them. You're a well-known man, am I right?" he said with a glance in Karl's direction. The girl nodded and left the room.

Weisenthal counted the money Karl had brought with him. Karl shifted his weight from foot to foot. He was vaguely embarrassed now at the considerable amount of money he'd brought with him, although Weisenthal showed no surprise at the wad of cash.

"I'm buying a First Class ticket on the Titanic," Karl offered. "I hope I brought enough. I understand it was expensive, even for this time."

Weisenthal turned away, still counting bills. "Twenty-eight Pounds Sterling for a First Class cabin, more if you want one of the suites." He looked up and fixed Karl with a look that was friendly, yet intense. "And *do* try to remember, Doctor Sander that you *are* here. You're part of the past now – none of this 'even for this time' business. Once you leave this lab, you'll be a citizen of 1912, just like the rest of us."

Karl was intrigued. "What do you mean?"

Weisenthal sat down at a desk and typed a number into the computer. "Most of the technicians that work here go back and forth through time. They commute, if you want to think of it that way. Every laboratory has to have at least one historian, though, someone who lives in the period and really gets to know the environmental and social nuances of the time. That's me." He glanced at the screen, then opened a large wooden box that sat on the desk. He put Karl's money into the box, then pulled out several piles of bills.

"I'm going to change your money into 1912 currency, about half English Pounds and half American Dollars. You can buy your ticket at Southampton, and when you get to New York, you won't have to find a currency exchange right away." He opened a drawer in the desk and rummaged around. He came up holding a leather wallet. He tucked the cash into the wallet and handed it to Karl.

"This is much more accurate than the one you were carrying. Of course, you can collect yours when you come back through."

"Well, I was planning on returning via the lab in Washington," Karl said, remembering Nikolas's advice.

"Hmm, that won't work then will it?" Weisenthal thought for a moment. "Can I send it back with one of our techs? They can leave it at the Ministry for you."

"Fine, I guess." The wallet was empty, but it was still his.

"I'll make sure your papers and ID get back safely too," Weisenthal promised. "Our return system has never lost anyone's papers."

Karl knew the reasoning behind this insistence on historical accuracy, but it made him nervous to be throwing away his identity. The young assistant came back into the lab, and he took his business cards from her with a silent sigh of relief. At least they were something to hold onto, something to prove he was really still Karl Sander.

The cards were disappointingly plain. They identified him as a Doctor of Medicine, and the assistant had dressed them up with a caduceus, but still, they looked awfully bare.

"These are kind of...well, boring, aren't they?"

Weisenthal shrugged. "People aren't as concerned with identity theft now as they are in the twenty-first century. Besides, once you get your ticket that will be all the ID you need. Weisenthal looked Karl over critically. "You'll pass," he nodded. "All the rest of your clothes are of a similar fashion, I noticed."

"All except for the formal dinner jacket. I thought I'd need that on a voyage like this."

"Good thinking," Weisenthal said. "This is serious stuff. The people here are very concerned with keeping up appearances. That goes triple for the upper class. They think you don't belong, they'll be on you like a pack of wolves." He shook his head, smiling. "I envy you, Doctor Sander, I really do. The maiden voyage of the Titanic! Sure wish I could go. Maybe one of these times I will."

His remark puzzled Karl. "What do you mean?"

"Come on, it's time travel! I've been here several times already. We historians find a time we like, and we settle down, so to speak. We work five years or so, then we go back to the beginning, five years earlier. The people around us never know the difference. Neat, huh?" he grinned.

"It is," Karl agreed. He took a deep breath. "Well, I guess I'd better get going."

"You'll be fine," Weisenthal said. "There's a nice hotel across the street, four-star quality. Spend the night there, get used to the time difference. In the morning, tell the manager to arrange a cab to take you to Waterloo Station. You can catch the Boat Train from there."

"Good." Karl hefted the trunk and followed Weisenthal to the door of the lab. He came out of the lab into a shop. Appropriately enough for the historian's disguise, it was a tailor shop. Karl made his way past the dummies and the racks of suits, and opened the front door of the shop. He hesitated for one long moment, then stepped out into the world of 1912.

The first thing that struck him was the noise. He had always thought of the past as a silent place, quiet, unmoving, like the stiff poses in old photographs.

But here, the streets of London were alive with sound. Horses pulling hansom cabs clopped past, children ran by him shouting, food vendors droned their jingles as they trudged along pushing their carts, or stood at street corners to hawk their goods.

A grubby newspaper boy held up a paper and yelled the headline, startling him. The bells of a nearby church tolled, marking the passing of an hour that, for him, was still a hundred and thirty years gone.

Karl shook his head, almost nauseated by the swirl and bustle of an earlier age. He crossed the street with his head down, barely looking up to avoid the horse and pedestrian traffic that flowed around him.

He reached the relative quiet of the hotel and checked in, grateful for the calm air of elegance. A bellboy came up to take his luggage, and Karl gratefully relinquished it. He followed the bellboy up the narrow, carpeted stairs to his room.

The bellboy left the trunk next to the bed and waited patiently while Karl dug through his pockets for a tip. Luckily, Weisenthal had had the foresight to throw in a couple of coins. He handed one of the coins to the boy. The boy's eyes widened when he saw the money, and he glanced up at Karl with a shy grin of thanks. Karl consoled himself with the thought that it was infinitely better to tip too much than too little.

The bellboy left, closing the door behind him, and Karl sat down on the bed with a groan. He wasn't hungry; although it was beginning to get dark outside, his body thought he'd eaten breakfast just a few hours ago. But his mind was reeling with fatigue from the trip. He locked the door, used the bathroom, undressed down to his underwear, and climbed into bed.

Karl had never had a problem sleeping in hotel room beds, but this was different. The feel of the sheets, the décor of the room, the sounds drifting up from the street below all reminded him that he was in a time alien to his own.

He turned over and punched the pillow, unable to sleep. He lay with his eyes open, thinking about the start of the voyage in the morning, thinking about trying to stop the ship of disease from reaching its destination. Nikolas's words came into his mind before he could stop them: "*The Zeitsehen machines were never meant to be used to change history.*"

Karl snorted and punched the pillow again, fluffing it savagely until he had a comfortable spot for his head.

Honestly, he thought as he finally drifted towards sleep. I'm not going to change history that much, am I? What will I be doing by stopping the anthrax plague? I'll be saving thousands of lives. No, I'll be saving a *million* lives. The United States will have their chance at greatness – if they have the guts to take it – and Lukas will get to meet his great-grandmother. What's the worst that could happen?

***

As Karl slept, he dreamed.

He was in a crowd, a sea of people who crashed and surged against a stage like waves on a rocky beach. He looked up at the podium where the crowd's attention was focused. A man stood there, lifting his clenched hands in exhortation, speaking like a tiger, whipping the audience into a frenzy.

Wave after wave of sound crashed against Karl as he was carried away into the crowd. The words were indistinct – "See haah! See haah!" – but the people were savage in their acclamation. He felt strong, powerful, swept up in the emotions of the speech. He thrust his right hand upwards, like a blade, in a jubilant salute. This was it! This was right! This was everything!

Then the dream shifted, and he was dreaming of Rosalinde. He held her in his arms, just like he had so many times before, but this was different. She was thin, so very thin, but it wasn't Rosalinde's slim athletic body in his arms. The Rosalinde he held was painfully emaciated. His soul was floating, sobbing, drowning in the desolation he could feel all around him. He could smell something sweet and horribly burnt at the same time. He gagged with revulsion without knowing why.

He looked up at the human skeletons that shuffled past him in twos and threes, their gazes blank and uncaring.

One of them was Weisenthal – Karl recognized him from the lab, but the tech was now just skin stretched over jutting bones. He tried to call to him, to ask for his help, but Weisenthal ignored him.

Karl knew he had to lift Rosalinde, had to get her to a doctor, and to a safe place where she could recover from whatever ailment was ravaging her. But he had no strength left. Even her wasted frame was too much for him to carry.

He slumped to the dirt, worn out by the effort of trying to lift her. He could feel her heartbeat under his hands, a fluttering against the bony cage of her ribs. Then the thready pulse faltered, and stopped. She stiffened in his arms, sighed once, then slumped against him. He raised his head and shrieked.

***

Karl came bolt upright, panting and sweating, from a dream he mercifully could not remember. For a few moments, he struggled with the disorientation that comes with waking up in a strange place. Then reality came back to him. He shrugged out from underneath the covers and reached for his shirt.

He ate breakfast in the dining room of the hotel while waiting for his cab. He still wasn't quite used to being a hundred and thirty years in the past. The food tasted fine to him, but he couldn't shake the feeling that the bread should be stale and moldy, the milk curdled, the fruit rotted into a shriveled, unrecognizable mess. He had to keep reminding himself that April 1912 was right now, not some faded, curling page in a forgotten calendar.

It wasn't until Karl got to Waterloo Station that the feeling began to straighten itself out for him. The familiar press of people waiting on the platform helped to anchor him in this new reality. He found himself watching the faces around him. These weren't stiff, sepia-toned mannequins in old-fashioned clothes. These were real people, as real as he was. The thought comforted him, and he began to relax.

The Boat Train pulled into the station with an ear-splitting hiss of steam, and slowly came to a stop. Karl bent and reached for the handle of his trunk, preparing to wrestle it up the steps to the railroad car, but a small hand on his stopped him.

"I'll get that 'un, guv'nor," the young porter said. Karl straightened, remembering his disguise as a gentleman.

He nodded stiffly, and allowed the porter to lug the trunk over to the baggage car. His luggage taken care of, he paid a passing newsboy a few pence for a paper to read on the train. Then he climbed into the First Class car and made his way to an empty seat.

Karl looked around at his fellow passengers, continuing to find reassurance in their humanity. Most of them looked at him with brief, incurious stares, then allowed their glances to slide away, just as he had done when riding the jet trains of his own time. As he settled into his seat, though, he felt the weight of a different gaze on him. He looked up.

A little girl was staring solemnly at him. Karl was seized with the sudden conviction that she knew he didn't belong. She knew, with the clairvoyance of youth, that he was trespassing in an era not his own. A shiver ran down his spine as he returned the girl's stare.

Then her mother bustled up and grabbed her hand. Chattering away, she led the child to a seat at the other end of the car. Relieved, Karl shook open the newspaper he had bought. He started to puzzle out the articles on the front page, translating slowly.

The train jerked and began to move. Karl put the paper down. He knew from experience that if he tried to read while the train was moving slowly, his stomach would rebel with a queasy, unsettled feeling.

To combat this touch of motion sickness, he looked out the window. The train rolled past the suburbs of London on its way to the coast. Red brick buildings flashed past, each with a tidy back yard. Flowers bloomed in the tiny, well-kept gardens. Karl saw tulips and daffodils, and several trees dripping white blossoms. The bursts of color and shades of green enchanted him.

Soon they had left the outskirts of London behind, and the train was chugging through the English countryside. The brick and slate of the city was gone. In its place were lovely half-timbered buildings with sturdy thatched roofs. They were nestled like fairy-tale cottages in rolling fields of green grass tinged purple with heather. Once Karl saw a flock of sheep coming up over a low hill, harried by a black and white bundle of fur and energy.

The train pulled into Southampton at 11:30, right on time. Karl folded the paper and stretched, hearing dull pops from his spine. He crabwalked to the end of the car, politely dodging the other passengers, and made his way down the steps.

He took a deep breath of the fresh air. After the smog of London, the bracing sea breeze of the port was welcome. A short walk brought him to the ticket office. A bell above the door jangled to announce his entrance, and the ticket seller looked up.

"Can I help you, sir?"

"Yes," Karl said, reaching for the wallet Weisenthal had given him. "I need passage aboard the Titanic. One-way."

"Which class?"

"First of course." Karl did his best to sound confident.

The ticket seller raised his eyebrows as he filled out the paperwork. "You're getting the last one, sir. In fact, the suites are completely booked. Have been for weeks. I trust a First Class stateroom will be sufficient?"

"Fine, fine," Karl said. He counted out the money and pushed it through the ticket window. The ticket seller nodded.

"Have a pleasant voyage, sir."

Karl collected his ticket and his luggage tag, and nodded his thanks.

On his way back to the train platform to find his steamer trunk, Karl had to skirt a growing crowd of people. More passengers were arriving, along with the friends and relatives that had come to see them off. Karl found his trunk and attached his luggage tag to it. Then he flagged down a porter to take it over to the growing mountain of baggage that waited to be loaded onto the ship.

Karl followed the milling crowd of people. Anticipation warred with anxiety as he peered over the heads of the people in front of him, straining for his first glimpse of Titanic.

Suddenly, there she was.

A wall of black steel rose in front of him, dotted at intervals with small portholes, and he realized he was looking at the hull of the ship. He craned his neck to look up the steeply sloping side.

Passengers stood at the rail, waving to the crowds below. Above them, starkly outlined against the sky, were four huge smokestacks. They were raked backwards, Karl noticed. Despite the massive bulk of the ship beneath them, the angle of the smokestacks gave the impression of speed, even when Titanic rode quietly at anchor. Waves lapped at the hull in a gentle rhythm. Seagulls wheeled and cried as they rode the breeze.

Karl stood and stared. How could he possibly have planned to stop this beautiful, horrible ship?

It felt like madness now even to try. Stopping this ship would be like shouting into the face of a hurricane, or trying to push an iceberg out of the way.

For one brief moment he thought of cashing in his ticket, taking the next train back to London, and returning to his own time.

He could be back home, with Rosalinde and Lukas, before Rosalinde's morning cup of tea was cool. The thought was enormously appealing, and his hand even stole into his jacket pocket to check for his ticket.

Then he remembered his assignment. He was still supposed to be studying the plague in America. It didn't matter how he got there, whether he travelled by Zeitsehen machine or by boat.

He'd paid for a First Class stateroom on the Titanic. He might as well enjoy the ride.

He started up the gangway, the metal echoing hollowly under his feet as he walked. He had reached the top and had just stepped onto the ship when he was jostled by somebody coming up behind him.

"'Scuse me," the man muttered, and brushed past him, clutching a pad of paper and a pencil. Before Karl could respond, the man had disappeared into the crush of passengers that filled the entryway. Karl pushed through the throng, thinking he'd lost the guy, but spotted him moments later.

"Captain Smith! Captain Smith, a word, please?" The reporter was waving, trying to get the attention of a distinguished-looking man in a spotless white uniform. The captain turned and noticed the waving reporter. His face, framed in a snow-white beard, creased into a friendly smile. Karl trusted him immediately.

"What can I do for you, young man?"

The reporter paused for breath. "Captain, would you care to make a statement for the press? You're commanding the Titanic on her maiden voyage, your last commission before retirement. How do you feel? Can you share your experiences with the world?"

Captain Smith half-closed his eyes, and the reporter waited, his pencil poised to scribble.

"When anyone asks me how I can best describe my experiences of nearly forty years at sea, I merely say uneventful. I have never been in an accident of any sort worth speaking about." He paused, stroking his lush beard. "I never saw a wreck and have never been wrecked, nor was I ever in a predicament that threatened to end in disaster of any sort."

The reporter nodded, scribbling furiously. He turned away, his head down, still writing, and came towards Karl.

Karl was about to tell the reporter to watch where he was going, but just then, the ship's whistles let loose three long blasts of sound. A stocky officer shouted, "All ashore that's going ashore!" The reporter looked up and blinked, finally aware of his surroundings. He hurried down the gangway. Karl let him go, and went to find his stateroom.

He found B Deck without too much trouble, and went down the hallway to his room. When he got there, he found a steward unpacking his steamer trunk. Karl breathed a silent sigh of relief that he had kept the BacFinder in his pocket instead of trusting it to the trunk.

The steward put the last neatly folded shirt into the clothes cupboard and shut the door. "There you are, sir, all squared away. We'll be pulling out shortly." Karl nodded, and the steward left the room. Karl looked around at the elegant stateroom that was to be his home for the next five days.

The room was paneled with wainscoting in a beautiful light wood, and above that, wallpaper in a muted shade of rose. A down comforter covered the large bed. Two fluffy pillows, sheathed in white pillowcases, beckoned silkily, even though it was barely past noon.

Karl was already looking forward to sinking into those pillows at the end of the day. Even though he knew the room had been designed for a whole procession of anonymous guests, there was a certain charm in knowing that he was the first person to stay in it. It felt almost as if the room had been designed and built solely for him.

A bright blast on a trumpet sounded in the hallway, calling the passengers to dinner. Karl followed the other First Class passengers to the dining saloon. He was looking forward to his first meal aboard ship. Breakfast had been hours ago, and he was famished.

A steward opened the door for him and bowed slightly as he went in. The room was brightly lit, and cheerfully and unrepentantly refined. The tables were arranged with space between them, so that dinner conversations could remain private.

Karl sat down at a table and hiked his chair closer. He wished he'd brought a book with him, rude as that might have been. He hated dining alone, and when he had to do it, the company of a good novel was the only thing that made it bearable.

"May we join you?" a voice trilled. Karl looked up to see a young woman in a frilly pale yellow dress. A man in a brown suit stood close behind her.

"Of course," Karl said. He stood as the man helped the woman with her chair, then he sat again when they were settled. "I was just hoping I wouldn't have to dine alone," he confessed.

"Oh, you needn't worry about that," the lady laughed. Her lilting accent was pure upper-class English. "They always set up the tables this way, to give people a chance to mingle. You can sit with your friends, or you can have different companions at every meal, if you wish. I find the variety fascinating, don't you, Charlie?"

The man in the brown suit nodded. "Quite, quite. You can never tell whom you'll meet at dinner on board one of these liners."

The meal was excellent, the conversation refreshing. Karl learned that his dinner companions were newlyweds, travelling to America for their honeymoon. "Niagara Falls. I can hardly wait!"

Karl almost asked them if Niagara Falls was anywhere near the East Coast, but then decided that it would be too awkward to explain why he'd asked. Besides, he reasoned, the less he messed with people's personal histories, the better off he'd be.

"Wasn't that near miss this afternoon something?"

Karl looked up from the roll he was buttering. "What do you mean?"

"Why, the Titanic almost colliding with the New York, that's what, for heaven's sake. Weren't you up on the boat deck as we left?"

Karl's throat was dry as he answered. "I had no one to see me off. I went straight to my stateroom and missed the castoff."

"Oh, it was horrifying, I tell you. I was standing there with Charlie, and we were waving at my aunt and my cousins on the dock. Suddenly there was a noise like...like..."

"Like gunshots," Charlie offered.

"Yes, I suppose you're right. The ropes holding the New York snapped right off."

"The swell of Titanic's engines had created a wave, you see, and lifted poor New York right out of her moorings. It was pure luck we didn't crash right there."

"Oh, no, not luck," the lady demurred. "I was talking with Captain Smith just before dinner. It was his quick thinking that saved the day. He ordered the engines reversed – hard! – and that swung the ship 'round enough so that the New York couldn't hit us."

"Yes, then several tugboats were able to slip in and guide New York back into her proper place, just like nursemaids herding an errant child back into line."

"Well, that was lucky." Karl tried to force a note of relief into his voice.

Inwardly, though, he was fuming. Why couldn't Captain Smith have been just a little slack in his duties?

A decision made a few moments later, and the Titanic wouldn't have sailed. The accident would have happened in full view of land, everyone on board would have been evacuated and gotten to shore safely, and his self-imposed mission to stop the ship from getting to America would have been over.

Why did Smith have to be so damned good at being a captain?

His dinner companion echoed his thoughts. "Isn't it amazing, that Captain Smith knew just what to do to save the ship?" she said in a dreamy voice.

"Oh ho, do I have a rival for your affections so soon, my love?"

"Never, Charlie, you know better than that." The newlyweds cooed at each other for a few moments. Karl excused himself. He'd had enough for one day.

The next day, Titanic stopped for a while at Queenstown, Ireland, to pick up mail and steerage passengers before setting off across the Atlantic.

Karl leaned on the rail and watched the Third Class passengers shuffle on board. He had the brief idea of wandering through the Third Class area with his BacFinder hidden up his sleeve, but promptly discarded the thought. The steerage passengers would all have undergone rigorous health checks before being allowed to board. No, his carrier would most likely be in First or Second Class.

That was the theory he was working with, that someone (or several *someones*) on the ship were carriers of anthrax, maybe even suffering in the first stages themselves.

He roamed the ship like a ghost, watching people as he passed, wondering which of them might be cultivating massive swarms of anthrax germs in the moist heat of their lungs.

Once, a Second Class child coughed loudly behind him. Karl spun around and nearly whipped out the BacFinder before he stopped himself.

He wandered over to the railing of the ship and looked out at the deep water. Titanic cut easily through the waves, leaving a foamy wake behind her. The regular splash of the waves at her side soothed him with its whisper.

He looked back at the spuming wake behind the ship. It reminded him how fast they were going, travelling without hesitation to their tragic destiny. The plague would strike, millions would die, and there was nothing he could do about it.

Karl found it hard to concentrate on the conversation at dinner that evening. Time was slipping away from him, like water through his fingers, and he was still no closer to finding the source of the anthrax plague, or to stopping the ship. He went to the Grand Saloon. He needed a drink, and some time to sort out his thoughts.

Soft strains of music greeted him as he came through the door. A band was playing in the corner of the room, and couples were dancing to the happy beat. He took a seat, and a waiter came over to take his drink order. Karl ordered a brandy, which came within moments.

As he sat sipping his drink, he became aware of someone watching him. He tried to ignore the feeling, hoping that whoever it was would lose interest in him. He didn't feel much like company tonight.

A female voice said, "Would you care to dance?"

Karl sighed and looked up.

He blinked. A strikingly beautiful woman was watching him from a few feet away, smiling. A dark green silk dress clung to the curves of her body, trailing behind her in a slight train. An embroidered spray of peacock feathers draped over her left shoulder. Light green gloves covered her slim hands and arms, almost to the elbow.

Karl had never seen a woman wearing gloves before, not in real life. The effect was stunning, almost erotic somehow. Another small peacock eye winked at him from the side of her reddish-gold curls, which were piled high on her head, cascading down in a fall of light onto her white shoulders.

Her cheeks were touched with pink, while her lips were a promising, pouting red. She was exquisitely beautiful, and she stood waiting for his answer.

"Would you care to dance?" she repeated. She tilted her head and smiled. Karl shrugged. He set his brandy down on the table, got up, took her hand, and led her to where the other couples were dancing.

Karl felt awkward at first, but he did know enough to lead. The woman seemed content to follow, moving her feet just enough to keep up with the gentle waltz. Karl realized that the chance for conversation was more important to her than a proper dance.

"I'm Daisy," she said by way of introduction.

"Daisy what?"

"Just Daisy will do for now," she smiled. "And you are?"

"Doctor Karl Sander," he said, unwilling to relinquish proper manners. He felt as though he was treading on dangerous ground, and a misstep could be nasty.

"You're German, aren't you?"

"How did you know?"

"Your accent. A lot of ladies have commented on it, if you weren't aware."

"I wasn't." Was his presence really attracting that much attention?

"Oh yes. It's very, how should I best put it: European. Very attractive to a simple countrified American like myself." Cool humor flashed in her eyes.

"Is that so?" Karl smiled. "Are all American women as forward as you are?"

"Oh, not nearly. A girl like me asking a man like you to dance? It's unheard of. Positively scandalous. But I figured that if I waited for you to ask me, I'd be waiting an awfully long time."

She moved closer, closer than she needed to for the steps of the dance. "I'm travelling alone too. Shocking, isn't it?"

"I suppose so." Karl had understood from his research that the morals of the early twentieth century were a lot stricter than this.

"I'm kidding, of course. I just say that to shock people. I'm travelling with my friend, Mr. Welles. He's the tall fellow standing over there by the potted plants."

She wiggled her fingers at the young man, who didn't notice.

"He's useful for helping me fend off the wrong kind of advances, and I can avoid awkward questions about my marital status when he's around. Other than that, there's nothing between us. We're each just as free as a little bird." She leaned into him. Her warm whisper tickled his ear. "You do understand, don't you?"

"Oh yes. I understand." He held her close, swaying with her, with the music. The light floral perfume she'd touched behind her ears intoxicated him more than brandy ever could. The waltz ended, and she took his hand and led him to the corner of the room.

"I enjoyed that," she stated. Her voice was low, musical, and almost breathless although she hadn't danced hard enough to exert herself. "Now what, Doctor Sander? Karl?"

Hearing his name on her lips brought Karl up short. He drew back a bit to look Daisy full in the face. Her eyes, he noticed, were a deep violet, long lashed, absolutely gorgeous. Hidden lust smoked in her gaze, and the curve of her full lips promised unimaginable delights.

"I wish..." she let the thought trail off, then blushed and glanced at him from beneath lowered lashes.

The look sent a dull heat through Karl's belly.

This was strange. From all he'd read about the morals and behavior of this time, he had imagined all the women to be straight-laced, proper models of decorum. He'd never in his wildest dreams imagined such a pretty little wanton as Daisy. But it would be death to his social standing on the ship to take her up on her unspoken offer. Already he could feel the eyes of half the people in the room upon him, their critical gazes boring into his back.

Besides, there was Rosalinde to think about. He had enjoyed dancing with Daisy, and that was fine. But betrayal of his wife in another century was still betrayal. He couldn't do that, not to Rosalinde.

There was one other thing to consider. Karl gazed at Daisy's full lips, imagined kissing them, imagined sinking into her and tasting her luscious heat. Even with thoughts of Rosalinde in his mind, he wavered, wanting Daisy. Then he made himself remember the BacFinder in his pocket. What if this gorgeous creature was one of his carriers?

What if her lungs were swarming with pulmonary anthrax germs right now?

Daisy seemed to sense his reluctance. She tossed her reddish-gold curls. “Never mind,” she said, forcing a quiet laugh. “It doesn’t matter what I wish, does it?”

Karl gave her a strained smile. “I’m just trying to be a gentleman.”

“I see.”

“I’m sorry,” he offered.

“No need to be.” She smiled politely, but Karl could sense the chilly disappointment lingering beneath the surface. She turned and walked away without another glance. Karl watched her go. A vague feeling of resentment washed through him. He left the lounge and headed for his stateroom.

He undressed and climbed into bed. He lay there in the darkness, missing Rosalinde and feeling sorry for himself. He had heard Titanic called ‘the ship of dreams’. That seemed to be true for everyone but him. For him it was a ship of nightmares. He was the only one who knew the chilling truth about Titanic and her deadly cargo.

He thought about Charlie and his new bride, enjoying their honeymoon. He thought about John Jacob Astor, who’d been pointed out to him yesterday as the richest man on the ship.

Astor was travelling with his new wife too, who was already expecting their child. Karl had lost track of the couples he’d noticed, holding hands as they strolled the promenades together, sitting close at dinner, sharing a cup of hot broth as they sat on the deck.

Everyone, it seemed was happy aboard this ship.

Everyone but him.

He heard footsteps coming down the hallway; then heard a gentle knock on the door. For one wild moment he imagined that Daisy was at the door. She'd somehow found his room, maybe followed him, and had just been waiting for the chance to offer herself to him again. He felt a surge of hope. Then a wave of disgust rolled over him as he thought of Rosalinde. Couldn't he even stay true to her in his thoughts?

Then he realized that the knock had not been at his door, but at the door to the room across the corridor. He heard a whispered conversation, then the soft sound of the door closing.

A sense of desolation overwhelmed him, and he turned over to hide his face in the pillow.

He missed Rosalinde, simply, powerfully. She was so far away, and there was nothing he could do to speed up the time. He had no choice – he had to suffer without her until he returned to his own time.

He consoled himself with the thought that no matter how long he stayed in 1912, he would be returning to 2037 at the moment he left it. He would be back in his own home for supper that evening, and Rosalinde wouldn't even have noticed his absence. As far as she was concerned, he would simply come home from work as usual. She wouldn't be suffering and lonely without him, the way he was now yearning for her. The thought, however, was cold comfort.

He still missed her desperately.

It took him a long time to fall asleep that night, and when he did, his pillow was wet with tears.

***

Karl was still feeling lonely and low the next day.

He was wandering around the ship without much of a plan, when he realized that he had found his way into one of the storerooms in the hold. The muted roar of the huge engines was noticeable down here, so close to the bowels of the ship. Karl wandered through the hold, eyeing the stacked baggage and supplies. Light gleamed off the glossy paint of a new Renault automobile. Karl ran a finger lightly over the smooth finish of the car, admiring the classic lines of the old fashioned design.

He moved over to a pallet of woolen blankets. The blankets were piled in a neat stack, awaiting the capable hands of a maid to smooth them down over a freshly made bed. Karl absently stroked the fine, light gray wool as his mind wandered.

A thought tickled the back of his mind. Somehow, he felt that there was something about the texture of the blanket under his fingers that was important. He relaxed, knowing that the answer would come to him if he didn't force it.

The thought took shape and grew as he played with the blanket, idly running the edge between his fingers.

Mentally he ran through what he'd read about anthrax. Pulmonary anthrax results from inhaling the spores of the anthrax bacterium.

The spores travel from the lungs to nearby lymph nodes, where they multiply. The lymph nodes break down and bleed, spreading the infection throughout the chest. Infected fluid builds up in the lungs and in the space between the lungs and the chest wall.

At first, the symptoms are vague, similar to influenza. Soon, though, the fever worsens, and in a few days, severe breathing difficulties develop. This is followed by vomiting, shock, and coma. In some cases, infection of the brain may also occur.

Pulmonary anthrax, also known as woolsorter's disease, is nearly always fatal.

Something fell into place in his brain with an almost audible click. Woolsorter's disease! He pulled the BacFinder out of his pocket and trained it on the pallet of blankets. The small blue screen glowed brightly enough to read by.

Karl had a moment of stark terror before he remembered that he'd been thoroughly vaccinated. He thought quickly. He had to find a way to get these blankets off the ship before they reached New York.

He examined the pallet of blankets closely. There was no way he could wrestle the entire pallet up the stairs and throw it overboard. He would just have to come down here over the next two days and smuggle the blankets up, several at a time.

First things first.

He noted the location of the pallet. It was the one off the left rear wheel of the Renault. Karl sprinted up the stairs and headed for his stateroom, walking quickly. In his stateroom, he rummaged through the desk until he found what he was looking for. Grabbing the bottle of ink, he went back down to the hold.

In front of the pallet, he pulled out the BacFinder again, just to make sure he had the right blankets. The screen still glowed blue in the dusk of the hold. Karl put the device away and unscrewed the top of the ink bottle. The chalky smell of the ink tickled his nose.

He upended the bottle over the pallet, marking the blankets with dark streaks and splashes of ink. The bottle was half empty by the time he realized he should have checked all the stores of blankets for anthrax. He quickly turned the bottle upright and fumbled the cap back on.

He heard footsteps coming towards him, echoing slightly in the space of the hold. He shoved the bottle into his pocket and wiped his fingers on the lining of his jacket. He moved away from the pallet, trying to draw attention away from the ink-streaked blankets.

A steward came up to him. "May I help you, sir? You seem to have lost your way, if I may be so bold."

"Yes, I guess I did. It's such a big ship, you know?" Karl laughed weakly.

The steward chuckled. "That it is, sir. I'll help you to your proper area, shall I?"

"Oh, that won't be necessary. I'll be fine."

"It's really no trouble at all. Right this way, sir."

Karl recognized the futility of trying to argue with such an implacable servant. He allowed the steward to steer him gently back topside to the café.

In the café, Karl ordered a drink, and sat thinking furiously. It seemed that his personal mission had changed. In a way, it was something of a relief. He no longer had to worry about stopping the mammoth Titanic. That, he now realized, had been a foolish idea. Now his task was much smaller, but no simpler. He had to find a way to get that pallet of blankets off the ship. But how?

He spent the next day skulking around the corridors on B Deck. Now that he had a plan, he wanted to go down to the hold again. His idea was to go down there, bring up a few blankets at a time, and quietly throw them overboard.

He had worked out a route in his head, one that would take him through the least populated areas of the ship.

Even with his plan, though, moving around unobtrusively on a ship with 2200 passengers was no easy thing. Also, every time he headed in the direction of the hold, he imagined he saw a steward or a maid watching him. They were very discreet, as they'd been trained to be, but their presence unnerved him. He spent the day in a fury of inactivity.

After dinner, Karl played cards with a few of the other men in the First Class smoking lounge. He wasn't big on card games, but he had to do something to keep his mind off those damn blankets.

"You're awfully quiet tonight, Doctor Sander," one of the men remarked as he picked up his hand.

"It's nothing," Karl said. "Just missing my wife."

"Ah. Is she in America?"

"No, I left her behind. In Germany."

"I see." The man took a puff on his cigar, then turned to the man sitting across from Karl. "What about you, Stead? Are you in on the pool? Ismay says we've made 519 miles today. He's betting we'll pull into New York on Tuesday rather than Wednesday."

William Stead, a short man with piercingly intelligent blue eyes, leaned back comfortably in his chair. "No, gentlemen, I'm not concerning myself with the pool. Everyone knows that the Titanic wasn't built to be an ocean greyhound, like the Mauretania or the Lusitania. The Titanic is the last word in luxury, gentlemen, not speed. Ismay would do well to remember that. After all, it is his ship."

"Hear hear," the man sitting next to Karl said. "More claret, if you please, waiter."

That night, while lying in bed trying to sleep, Karl had an idea. He knew that wireless technology was still in its infancy. The Marconi set on the Titanic was top of the line as far as equipment went, but he'd be willing to bet that even the Titanic's wireless machine was slow and balky. If he could find a way to sabotage the radio, perhaps the Titanic would have to slow down to make repairs, no matter how Ismay might bluster.

The next afternoon, Karl went up to the wireless room to test his theory. He passed Captain Smith and Bruce Ismay in the hallway, and slowed down just a bit to listen to their conversation.

"I've gotten another ice warning, Mr. Ismay. This one's from the Baltic."

"Really? Let me see it."

Karl heard the crisp crackle of a piece of paper being passed from one man to the other.

"Hmm," Ismay said. "Interesting."

Karl looked around in time to see Ismay stuff the message into his pocket.

"This will make stimulating dinner conversation, I'm sure. Don't you worry about it, Captain. I'm sure you can handle anything that should arise." Ismay clapped Smith lightly on the shoulder and walked off down the hallway. Karl continued on his way to the wireless room, thinking over the exchange he'd just witnessed.

He knocked at the open door of the wireless room. "Excuse me, but may I come in?"

"You and the rest of First and Second Class," the man at the table grumbled. "What's this message going to be? 'Having a great time, wish you were here'?"

"Actually, I'm not here about a message. I was wondering if you could tell me a little about how the wireless set works."

The man let out a long-suffering sigh. "Quickly?"

"Yes, if you don't mind."

"Quickly, then. Electricity flows into the telegraph key on one end, and is interrupted when the operator taps a message in Morse code. Ultimately, the voltage is turned into electromagnetic waves, then transmitted over an antenna. Got it?" The man peered up at Karl, obviously hoping he had bored his unwelcome visitor into cutting his stay short.

"Sounds interesting," Karl lied, trying to think of some excuse to prolong his visit. He had to find some way to sabotage the wireless set, but he couldn't very well just ask the Marconi operator to leave the room while he did it.

Captain Smith unwittingly came to Karl's aid. "Mr. Phillips? Would you bring me the messages from Cape Race, please?" he called from the hallway.

"Coming, Captain." Phillips took off his headphones and grabbed a stack of papers off the desk. He brushed past Karl and stepped out into the hallway.

Karl moved cautiously to the desk, keeping his body between the wireless machine and the still-open door. He grabbed a handful of wires at the back of the set and yanked hard. He felt some of the wires give, and decided that was good enough. Anything more would look like direct sabotage. He stepped away from the machine as Phillips came back into the room. He nodded at the young operator and left.

That afternoon, as Karl leaned against the ship's rail, still waiting for his chance to dump the infested blankets, he heard a Second Class couple discussing the rumors of ice warnings.

That got him thinking. If the Titanic was heading into a field of icebergs, surely the ship shouldn't be going as fast as it was. Perhaps he had done everyone on board a favor by forcing the ship to slow down. He looked down at the water purling away under the cutting hull, and tried to imagine the wreck that would happen if Titanic ran into an iceberg going at this speed.

He shivered. That was a thought best left alone.

Karl dressed carefully for dinner that night. He was getting discouraged, and he hoped that the elegant dinner would cheer him up. He was beginning to recognize many of the faces he saw at the dinner tables, and he was looking forward to good conversation. Perhaps he would even see Daisy.

Daisy *was* there, in red silk tonight, on the arm of a gentleman much younger than Karl. She caught sight of Karl, looked down. She even had the grace to blush, even though it just made her that much prettier. Karl suppressed a sigh, and sat down to dinner.

The food was excellent, as it had been the entire voyage.

Big baskets of fresh fruit dominated the tables, red apples and ripe yellow pears piled high, grapes dripping sensuously down the sides. Cheeses of every kind beckoned from silver plates on each table.

There were hors d'oeuvres, followed by soups, followed by poached salmon. The pink steak was decorated with a line of light cream sauce, with a cucumber fan on the side for garnish, and it looked absolutely delicious. Karl, who didn't care for fish, decided that he at least had to try the salmon. He was pleasantly surprised.

The entrée was even more stunning. The filet mignon was served on a bed of thinly sliced fried potatoes, with a buttery wine sauce encircling the plate. Karl sighed with pleasure as he lifted the first forkful of steak and potatoes to his mouth. The wine sauce brought out the rich taste of the meat, and the potatoes gave an interesting mealy texture to each bite.

Next to come was lamb with mint sauce, one of Karl's favorites, and a sirloin of beef. Two more potato dishes, green peas, and carrots in a cream sauce accented the meat. Rice served to round out the course. Sorbet cleansed the palate, and then it was on to the next onslaught of food.

A roast and a salad followed, and then a cold dish of foie gras. By the time the sweets course came, all Karl could do was look at the offerings and groan. He only wished he had room for chocolate painted éclairs, or French vanilla ice cream, or Waldorf pudding. The fan of peaches on a bed of pale green Chartreuse jelly looked quite lovely, but Karl was too stuffed even to think about dessert. He sipped a glass of champagne and wondered where these people put it all.

After dinner, when he finally felt like moving again, Karl went back up to the wireless room. As he approached the open door, he heard the rapid electronic clicks of the Marconi machine. He peered into the room. Phillips was sitting at the desk, jotting down messages. He looked up and saw Karl.

"Oh, it's you again."

"You look busy."

Phillips went back to his recording. "Wireless set was on the blink. I just now got it working. If you're wanting to send a message, it'll be a while. I'm rather backed up at the moment."

"Did we slow down at all? Lose any time?"

Phillips glanced up with a grin. "You're in the pool, huh? No, I'm happy to say we're making excellent time."

Karl was at a loss. On one hand, he was relieved that his little act of sabotage hadn't done permanent damage to the wireless. On the other – well, dammit, he hadn't even slowed the ship down, much less stopped it so he could take care of that business with the infected blankets. He picked up a stack of papers and began flipping idly through it.

One paper caught his attention, and he held it up to get a better look. It was from the Atlantic Transport liner Mesaba. "Lat. 42 N to 41.25 N, Longitude 40 W to 50.30 W, saw much heavy pack ice and great number large icebergs, also field ice."

Karl shuffled the papers. More ice warnings. He cleared his throat.

"Shouldn't the captain be shown these ice warnings? Maybe he'd give the order to slow down."

Phillips swung around in his chair. "Look, if you're trying to be some voice of doom here, forget it. The captain's in charge of the speed, and he's doing an excellent job. He always has. Those ice warnings will get to the bridge in their own time. Now, if you've got a message to send, I'll take it. If not, kindly leave, let me do my job, and let Captain Smith do his. Fair enough?"

Karl nodded and swallowed around the lump in his throat, and backed out of the wireless room.

He found a card game already in progress in the First Class lounge. Stead saw him and called out, "Doctor Sander! Join us, won't you? We wouldn't usually play cards on the Lord's Day, but on a maiden voyage, we'll make an exception."

Karl ordered a brandy from a passing waiter and sat down. He accepted the hand he was dealt, and tried to put the blankets out of his mind. He'd done the best he could. The Titanic was steaming along towards America and its destiny. There was nothing, nothing Karl could do to change that.

A while later, as the men sat playing cards, a slight bump seemed to shiver through the ship. It was gone as quickly as it had come. Stead looked up from his cards, and Karl frowned as he laid down a pair of tens. The moment passed.

Karl reached for his glass and found it empty. He signaled the waiter to bring him another drink. The waiter hurried up with another brandy and set the glass down at Karl's elbow. As Karl reached for it, he noticed something strange.

The level of brandy in the glass was slightly tilted.

He looked across the table at Stead, who shrugged and looked back down at his hand. Karl stood up from the table.

"Think I'll go for a stroll on deck."

"I believe I'll go with you," another man said. "Just to get some fresh air, you know."

"Better put on your greatcoats, boys. I hear it's plenty cold out there, just a few degrees above freezing."

Karl followed the other man out onto the deck. There were a few other people out on the promenade. They passed two women who were chatting excitedly.

"They say we've hit an iceberg! I wonder if there's any damage?"

Karl's companion nudged him. Three men were playing football with large chunks of ice that had fallen onto the deck.

"I'd say it looks like the only damage was done to the berg."

Karl looked over the side to the black water below. "Then why are we stopped?"

"Don't know. The captain's probably just seeing what's what. Soon as you know it, we'll be on our way again."

"I expect you're right." Karl shivered, even though he knew with the hindsight of history that the man was correct. Something felt...off, just...it felt wrong. Karl looked up at the sky.

Millions of stars twinkled and shone in the black velvet, and were reflected back in the inky black water. Karl felt the dizzying sense of standing in the middle of the universe, at the crossroads of time. He dragged his gaze from the hypnotic sky with an effort of will.

He happened to glance up at the boat deck. What he saw there sent a chill down his spine that had nothing to do with the frigid night air.

"Look at that! It looks like they're loading people into lifeboats."

His companion snorted. "Now *that's* a waste of time and energy. Everyone knows the Titanic's unsinkable. I'm going back inside, it's freezing out here."

"You're right. Let's go inside." As he followed the man back into the First Class lounge, Karl felt the smugness of the time traveler wrap around his mind like a comforting cocoon.

Of course the Titanic was unsinkable.

He knew that even the head-on collision of 1934 hadn't done enough damage to sink her. Why should a little brush with an iceberg worry him?

As he turned to shut the door, Karl had an idea. Titanic was stopped for the foreseeable future. Stewards and maids were bustling around tending to nervous passengers. Now would be the perfect time to go down to the storeroom and fling the blankets over the side. He could take all the time he needed, while running just a small risk of being seen. Then, when the ship got underway again, the danger would be gone. He would have done what he had set out to do. The thought galvanized him.

"I'll be back in a while, gentlemen. Don't hold the game up on my account."

Karl pushed his way through the crowds of people to the bow of the ship. He had mapped out the quickest way to the hold days ago, but it still took him half an hour to get there.

Everyone seemed to be wandering around the ship in a daze, as though they were actors who had forgotten their lines and were waiting for their cues.

Karl passed the group of musicians that had played in the saloon the night he and Daisy had danced together. Someone had dragged the upright piano out onto the deck, and the musicians were grouped around it playing. Karl recognized the Maple Leaf Rag. Some of the passengers had gathered to listen to the bright ragtime music. People were nodding and clapping in time, and one man grabbed his wife for a quick dance. Karl hurried past them. Right now he had more important things to do.

He reached the stairs that led to the storeroom and started down them. Something was wrong with the stairs, and he grabbed at the handrail to keep from falling. Then he realized what was throwing off his balance.

The stairs were tilted to the left.

He kept going, slowly and carefully. He reminded himself to pay attention to the new slant of the stairs. He didn't want to trip with an armload of blankets and twist his ankle.

He was almost at the bottom of the stairs before he realized that the last few steps were under water. He bent, hands on his knees, and peered into the hold. The storeroom was already under several feet of water, and he could see more pouring in from the rent in the hull. Boxes and bags floated past him, some sinking as they became waterlogged. He could see no sign of his marked blankets.

He felt something cold and wet on his feet, and looked down. The green water lapped greedily at his shoes. While he'd been standing there, the water had moved another few inches up the next step. He hastily backed away and ran up the crazy tilted steps.

At the top of the stairs, he took a deep, calming breath. Obviously the damage was worse than he thought. He could tell that the Titanic was going to fill with water and sink several feet, to ride at a lower level in the water.

As far as he knew that was what had happened in 1934. Still, he wasn't comfortable knowing that the ship was at a dead stand-still in the middle of the North Atlantic. "Careful what you ask for, my boy," he muttered. "Looks like you just got it."

He squished back to the lounge. The men were still there. Stead had abandoned the card game and was sitting in a leather chair in the corner, engrossed in a book. Karl saw that Clarence Moore and Frank Miller were still in the game. He sat down heavily in the nearest chair.

"Well, Sander? What did you find?" Miller took a drag on his cigar and blew out a puff of fragrant smoke.

"We're sinking." Karl couldn't seem to find any other words to describe the situation.

Stead looked up from his book, licked his fingertip, turned a page, and went back to reading.

Moore looked over at Major Archie Butt, who drawled, "Well, I'm not so sure about that. Titanic is unsinkable, you know. We'll probably just ride here for a bit until the sun comes up, then hail another ship and be towed to Nova Scotia for repairs."

Karl forced a note of calm into his voice. "I suppose you're right."

"Of course I am, young man," Major Butt assured him. "And even if, in the remote possibility that we do end up sinking, why, expressing alarm is not the way to behave on a foundering ship, is it, gentlemen?"

"Quite right, quite right, Major," the answers came back.

"After all, we do have the women and children to think about, don't we?"

"Of course, yes, that's absolutely true," came the soft chorus.

Karl got up stiffly from his chair. He felt as if he had suddenly been transported to a fancy dress ball in Hell. The realization dawned on him that the Titanic was indeed sinking. No one could look into that insidiously filling hold and not realize the awful truth.

"Please excuse me, gentlemen." Karl forced himself to walk quietly to the door, even though all his instincts were screaming at him to run. But really, where would he have run to? He was on a sinking ship in the middle of the cold, dark Atlantic. There was nowhere to go but down.

Out on the deck, Karl wandered aimlessly, taking in the sights of the unfolding tragedy. The band was still playing ragtime, although some of the audience members were beginning to look around fearfully.

Across the ship on the Boat Deck, lifeboats were being loaded with women and children. Karl looked at the boat that was being lowered, bumping its way slowly down the side of the boat towards the black water below. Then he looked back at the silent masses of people that were waiting for their turn. His eyes widened as a sickening thought occurred to him.

There weren't enough lifeboats.

There never had been. Any idiot could have seen that. Sixteen boats, four collapsibles. Fine and dandy. Two thousand, two hundred passengers and crew. It didn't take a rocket scientist – or an infectious diseases specialist – to do that horrible math.

Karl walked slowly back towards the lounge. As he passed the café, he glanced inside. The restaurant was cheerily lit, but empty. As Karl watched, the tall water glasses sitting on the tables wobbled, then tilted forward. First one fell. Then another. Then another.

Karl reached the promenade outside the lounge, fighting his way against the increasing tilt of the deck. He tried to ignore the frightened voices of the other passengers, a growing whirlpool of sound that threatened to suck him under with cries of despair.

He stood outside the lounge for several long moments, gripped in an agony of indecision. Which would be better, to be inside the ship when it sank, or outside? The physician in him weighed the choices.

Inside, his lungs would implode before the ship was twenty feet down. It wouldn't be a painless death, but at least it would be quick. Or should he stay on deck and try to swim away from the ship? There was always the chance he would be picked up by one of the lifeboats.

The ship lurched forward, and Karl was thrown to his knees. A mighty bellowing groan came from the middle of the ship, along with a horrendous crash and the shriek of stressed metal. Something deep in Titanic's guts had broken. The deck tilted nearly upright, and Karl grabbed for the rail. He started climbing towards the stern of the ship.

The lights flickered; then went out. Karl kept climbing in the dark, ignoring the prayers and pleas for help that rose around him. At last he reached the stern. He climbed over the rail and stood on it, feeling the huge ship shudder underneath his feet. Not long now. He looked down, down, down to the blackness below. Water dripped from the massive propellers. His stomach did a queasy flop as he realized that those propellers should never have been that far up in the open air.

Then the ship lurched again, and began to slide slowly into the water. A fist gripped Karl's heart and squeezed. He clenched his eyes shut tight; then opened them. He wouldn't go to his death with his eyes closed. The black water came nearer and nearer. Karl took a deep breath, trying to prepare himself for the plunge into the icy depths.

In the end, Titanic slipped gently into the sea. A few bubbles rose up as she went gracefully under the surface, a lady to the end. Karl felt the deck rail leave his feet under the water.

Then he gasped as the shock of the icy water took his breath away. Moments later, the pain hit him. The pain ate at him, gnawed all the way down into his bones. His breath came faster, ruffling the water in front of him. He could see fist-sized chunks of ice floating with him in the water.

Tears squeezed from his eyes and trickled down his face. He could feel them freezing to his skin. His bones had been replaced with icy white hot rods of searing, solid pain.

Karl chewed on his lip, trying to fight the cold and the pain. He tasted cold blood on his tongue. He grabbed at a lifebelt that was floating past, and clung to it. He could hear the screams and moans of the dying all around him in the darkness. He closed his eyes, trying to relax, to get used to the cold. Soon, though, he was screaming himself. The cold forced high, breathy shrieks from him as it sucked his life away.

Gradually, his scream tapered off into harsh moans. He swallowed freezing salt water, gagged, and tasted blood. His throat was raw, and it felt like something inside was ripped. At least the sound around him seemed to be dying down. That was a relief.

Karl closed his eyes, still shaking with the cold. He saw a light behind his closed eyelids, and heard a voice calling him.

"Karl? Karl. Wake up, sweetie, it's Grandma."

Karl opened his eyes and saw his grandmother. She was healthy, smiling, not wasted and gaunt like the last time he'd seen her. Behind her he could see the back yard. Sunlight filtered through the trees and touched her face with radiant health. On her lap she held a small boy. Karl recognized the boy's outfit. He'd worn a pair of red shorts and a striped shirt like that when he was four years old.

His grandmother waved to him, and waved the little boy's arm too. "Come back to us soon, Karl. I'll be waiting for you."

Karl reached for the light, aching to see his grandmother again. He blinked, and the sunlight faded into a tight white beam. "Is anyone alive out there?" he heard faintly across the water. He raised his arms and slammed them weakly into the water, hoping the caller could hear his feeble splashing efforts.

A lifeboat rowed slowly into sight, and Karl's face cracked in a grin. "Thank God," he croaked. "You're here."

A crewman reached over to grab his hands. "Yes, friend, we're here. Come on, let's get you into the boat and warmed up."

Strong hands helped Karl into the boat. He sat on the wooden bench shivering. He couldn't believe his luck. He was alive. He was going to go home.

"Here, give this to him. Poor man." A woman handed the crewman a wool blanket to drape over Karl's shoulders. The crewman shook it out and handed it to Karl, who stared at the blanket in horror. A splash of dried ink marked the light gray wool. Karl flinched and moaned.

Then blackness swam over him, and he fell into it with a sigh.

***

April 29, 1912.

From the transcript of the investigation into the Titanic disaster, Senator William Alden Smith, presiding.

Smith: Joseph Boxhall, you were the fourth officer on the ship, in charge of Lifeboat Number Two. Did you go back for anyone after the sinking?

Boxhall: Yes sir, the lifeboat I was commanding did return.

Smith: Were you able to rescue any souls from the water?

Boxhall: Yes, we pulled one man, a German, into the boat, but he expired shortly afterwards.

Smith: Did he die from the cold?

Boxhall: Yes sir, I believe he did. We offered him one of the blankets that were in the boat, but he thrust it away from him, as if it were – I don't know – diseased.

Smith: Interesting. Was there anything particular about these blankets you had in the boat, anything that could have excited the German's revulsion?

Boxhall: No sir, not at all. One of the stewardesses had brought an armload of blankets onto the lifeboat with her. I assumed they were from one of the First Class linen closets.

Smith: Thank you. Officer Boxhall, you are dismissed.

"History is the version of past events that people have decided to agree upon."
Napoleon Bonaparte

"To my poor fellow-sufferers: My heart overflows with grief for you all and is laden with sorrow that you are weighed down with this terrible burden that has been thrust upon is. May God be with us and comfort us all."
Eleanor Smith (wife of Captain Smith)

"Hell is truth seen too late."
Thomas Hobbes, Leviathan

BIOGRAPHIES

NERINE DORMAN

Nerine subsists on gourmet coffee, and spends most of her day unfucking sentences, making words, and pushing little picture boxes around on screens. She freely admits to having impure thoughts about Varric Tethras. Stalk her on Twitter @nerinedorman.

DEAN M. DRINKEL

Author, Editor, Poet, Award Winning Script-Writer, Theatre & Film Director.
More about Dean can be found at: http://deanmdrinkelauthor.blogspot.co.uk/, www.ellupofilms.com and Issue 331 of Fangoria.

D.T. GRIFFITH

David could write a happy story as long as it ends with someone dying or falling into a pit of self-loathing and derangement. He draws inspiration from classic and modern works of noir, dystopia, horror, and other dark fiction, weaving those elements into his own brand of storytelling. Educated in fine arts and creative writing, he has led a productive career in the creative and communication fields. He can be found sharing his thoughts on writing, books, and the world at large at www.dtgriffith.com and as @dtgriffith on Twitter.

JAMES POWELL - Cover Artist

As a child, artist James was very much afraid of the dark. It wasn't until his early teens that his mind twisted, and he became attracted to the horror genre. He's lived in the backwoods of the Deep South most all his life, which have provided inspiration for many of his dark and surreal works. He's worked with authors Neil Gaiman, Brian Hodge, Scott Nicholson, John Prescott, Joe R. Lansdale, and many others. He has done design work for actor Lance Henriksen, and horror punk legends the Misfits, and his art has recently appeared in the pages of Fangoria magazine. Being a native of Mississippi, and having a fondness for the Blues, he's often had to deny rumours about visiting crossroads and having dealings with the Devil. However, at the age of thirteen he did play in a fresh-dug grave. You can find out more at www.greyhaven.weebly.com, and www.facebook.com/artistjp.

KYLE RADER

The author of over fifteen short stories, of which *The Briny Deep* is his latest, Kyle is someone who doesn't like to color within the lines. He writes across multiple genres with the expressed goal of doing the unexpected and, above all, not boring his readers. He lives in New Hampshire and enjoys playing guitar poorly, yelling at his television, and, when time permits, the occasional skylark. He can be found online at kylerader.net.

SYLVIA SHULTS

Sylvia has been fascinated with the story of the Titanic ever since learning about the doomed liner in grade school. She writes both horror fiction and paranormal nonfiction. She has been a paranormal investigator for several years, and is the author of the acclaimed Fractured Spirits: Hauntings at the Peoria State Hospital. She has made many media appearances, including a spot on Ghost Hunters. Her collection of horror short stories, The Dark at the Heart of the Diamond, is available from Crossroad Press. Her nonfiction book Hunting Demons: A Ghost Hunter's Encounter With Evil will be available in 2015 from Whitechapel Press. She invites readers to visit her on Facebook and at www.sylviashults.com

ROBERT W. WALKER

Award-winning author and graduate of Northwestern University, Robert created his highly acclaimed *Instinct and Edge Series* between 1982 and 2005. Since then he has penned his award-winning historical series featuring Inspector Alastair Ransom with *City For Ransom* (2006), *Shadows In The White City* (2007), and *City Of The Absent* (2008), and most recently placed Ransom on board the Titanic in a hybrid historical/science fiction epic entitled *Titanic 2012 – Curse of R.M.S Titanic*. Rob then penned *Bismarck 2013 – Hitler's Curse, The Edge of Instinct, The Fear Collectors,* several YA titles and several short story collections. He is also responsible for the *Bloodscreams Series* and the historical suspense *Children Of Salem* - romance amid the witch trials. Robert currently resides in Charleston, West Virginia with his wife, children, pets - all somehow normal. He has three Facebook pages and a Twitter page. more on his published works an be found at www.robertwalkerbooks.com & www.amazon.com/kindlebooks.